I0570364

KASTLE LAW

CHRIS COPELAND

SOLE PUBLISHING LLC
Paperback Edition

CHRIS COPELAND

KASTLE LAW

ISBN: 978-0-615-21805-2

Printed in the United States of America

Published by Sole Publishing, P.O. Box 281, Tylertown, Ms 39667

Paperback Edition

What would you do if your lifelong dream was taken from you... if there were easy money only fingertips away... if you came face to face with a terrorist that had killed someone you loved? This is what I did...

CHAPTER 1
A Curveball

Sometimes in life, there are moments that happen that change your life forever; in that instant your simple, happy-go-lucky life goes in a totally different direction. My course was altered by a news announcement on the radio; I can remember every word like I heard it five seconds ago. "This morning a bomb exploded in downtown Jacksonville; killing a large number of people. A sense of panic and sadness has spread across the country. Who would do this? Why would they do this? Every American is demanding to have these questions answered on this tragic day."

My immediate reaction was one of disbelief, hurt, and rage. "She was there, she's gone." I began to go numb; anger took over every ounce of my being. Revenge was my only thought. "They will pay for this!" I'm sure everyone who lost someone that day had the same feelings that I did, but there were only a few who got an opportunity to do something about it.

I am getting ahead of myself; let me start from the beginning. I was born Kastle Benton Raines. My wonderful and amazing mother gave me a name that was unique to set me apart from everyone else. At least that is what she told me after a school day of being harassed and picked on. She always said that I was going to be great one day and I would put my stamp on the world in some shape or form. I heard this from her so much; therefore, at an early age I started believing every word that she said. My mother wanted me to make a difference. Perhaps become President or something like that, but my passion was sports. As much as I loved surfing, I later realized that baseball would be my ticket to success. I am just like everyone else; I want to win and I crave success. Once I saw dollar signs in my reach, surfing became an occasional hobby; which prevented any unnecessary injuries.

After high school, I had every college in the country recruiting me; I was a pitcher that could throw in the mid 90's. I loved standing on that mound, dominating the opposing hitters that were 60 feet in front me; it was the best feeling in the world. To the dismay of my parents, I decided to skip college and go for my dream by signing a minor league contract. In fact, I still have the picture that was taken on the day that I was drafted. It was of me proudly holding up the #5 Dodgers' Jersey. I was selected fifth overall in the draft by the Los Angeles Dodgers; at the time it was unheard of for a high school player to be drafted that high. I did not have to take the number 5, but that is the number I ultimately chose. Who knew how significant that number would eventually become?

My parents were disappointed; but, of course, I was so excited and overjoyed with the signing bonus and contract that I received. Plus, it was a chance to play for my hometown team. I grew up not too far from L.A. in Oceanside, California. My parents eventually got over the heartbreak of me foregoing higher education after my first minor league season. They could only come to a handful of games, but I talked to them after every one.

In my first five years, I was very successful when I was able to play. I had many injuries resulting in three arm surgeries. I started at Single A and made my way up to Triple A. Because of the frustrating injuries, I had been stuck in the minor leagues and held back from the majors.

With my Major League window starting to close, I had a great start at the beginning of my sixth year; and it was my second season with a Double A team, the Jacksonville Suns. I won my first three games without giving up a single run and in the fourth game of the year; I pitched the game of my life. I threw a no hitter; which I had never done before. I only allowed one person to reach base and I was one strike away from pitching a perfect game. To this day, the only pitch I remember is the one that was called a ball that prevented me from achieving perfection. I thought it was a strike and every time I replay it in my mind, I come to the same conclusion. Instead of dwelling on the umpire's incompetent call, I let myself enjoy that incredible moment. I was on top of the world, at the peak of my professional career. I felt like all of my dreams were about to come true. Finally, everything was coming together, or so I thought. As it turned out, that was the final game I ever played in.

After the game, I just had to go and celebrate. I brought my car home and called for a cab to take me to a nightclub. I would always do that, when I knew I was going to go out and drink; and this was definitely a night to celebrate. I always tried to stay out of trouble and I did not want to do anything to jeopardize my baseball career. Especially on that particular night; I was on the brink of my life long dream. The person from the cab company heard the game on the radio and sent a limo instead. I was very grateful to the dispatcher for providing the limo; after that, I felt it was truly my night.

I was going to Club Diamond, the premier nightclub in Jacksonville, which was located not too far from the stadium. The inside of my favorite post game hangout is set up like a baseball field. There are two long bars in place of dugouts and there is a big dance floor that is surrounded by bright green neon lights, where the outfield would be. It was the place to be on a Thursday or any night after a game.

When I arrived at the club, there was a long line to get in. The Mplants were having a concert on Saturday, so without a doubt it was a given that the most popular band in the world would make an appearance at the city's hottest club. The limo pulled up beside a white Mercedes convertible that was about to be valet parked. I had not been dating at the time; there was just a long line of the once in a while hook ups and occasional one night stands. The plan for that night was not any different; I wanted to celebrate, have a good time, and get laid. As I got out of the limo, I noticed two beautiful women get out of the Mercedes. The driver was wearing a baseball cap and I love an occasional baseball cap on a woman; I think that is so sexy. My heart stopped as soon as I saw her, but I had to play it cool.

"Nice car!" I said, as she was closing her car door.

"Thank you," she replied.

"I love your cap! You have good taste; I like the Suns too."

"I just came from the game; I didn't have enough time to go home and change," she quickly responded.

"Yeah, I was there; it was a great game wasn't it," I said to her with a great deal of enthusiasm; after cracking a smile.

"It was amazing!" She replied as we were walking toward the club. The door attendant spotted me and caught us before we could get to the enormous line. He shook my hand and told me that the owner wanted me to join him in the VIP section. I told him the only way I would go if they had room for two more.

"Sure, we do!" The door man eagerly and politely responded.

"I appreciate it; thank you man," I said, as I shook his hand.

"Would you ladies like to come with me?" I asked the two hot girls.

"Yes, thank you so much." The two women quickly and enthusiastically accepted my invitation. The door attendant had two bouncers escort us to the VIP area, where the owner had a big surprise waiting for me. The bouncers brought us to a small stage, in the middle of the club, where the club dancers were. The music was stopped and a spotlight was put on me; and then the DJ proceeded with a humbling introduction: "We have a special guest in here tonight. He is the best pitcher on the planet and has just thrown a no-hitter. From your Jacksonville Suns; the future major leaguer, Kastle Raines!" It was truly amazing; really, one of the best moments of my life. I have always loved introductions in all sports, even wrestling. The cool intro music is worth the price of admission. I have to see the introductions when I watch a game or a fight; it is awesome. I finally got off the stage after enjoying several minutes in the spotlight. When I did, I walked over to the sexy girl with the hat and spoke into her ear.

"I'm sorry for the interruption; I may never have a moment like this again, I had to enjoy it." I caught a whiff of a stimulating smell coming from her neck as I pulled away after speaking to her.

"I feel bad that I didn't recognize you. Actually, I'm a pretty big fan; seeing you without your baseball cap threw me off. You were so great tonight; it was the best game I have ever been to. I have been to a couple Yankee games with my dad but, they were nothing like this one," she sincerely said.

"How could you like the Suns and not like the Dodgers?"

"The Dodgers don't have Derek Jeter," she replied with a smile.

"No they don't. So, Yankee Fan! What's your name?"

"Sarah Newman, it's nice to meet you," she answered.

"No, the pleasure is all mine," I replied. The bouncers escorted us to the VIP area and the owner met us as soon as we got there. As he shook my hand, I introduced him to Sarah and her friend Naomi. He introduced us to his other guests, the Mplants. It was exciting for me to meet some famous rock stars like them; they were really cool and down to earth. Up to that point I had not met any famous people with the exception of a few well-known baseball players. Naomi hung out with the band most of the night, while Sarah and I were getting to know each other. Sarah and I had fun all night; we danced, talked, and did a little drinking too. I never thought I would have that much fun with a 24-year-old schoolteacher. Where was she when I was in school? The majority of my high school teachers were all pushing fifty or older, although they were excellent educators and taught me a lot.

At the end of the night, she told me that she had to get up early to meet her dad for breakfast. She gave me her number and we parted ways; which definitely was not the ending that I had in mind for the best day of my life. However, I actually felt good. It seemed like there could possibly be a future there and I had not felt like that in quite a while.

It was almost 2:00 A.M. and everyone who was around me was smashed. I had enough and it was time to call it a night; so I went outside to wait for the limo. My wonderful night had come to an end! When I got outside, after only a few seconds, I heard some screaming and other noises coming from the parking lot. I walked closer to get a better view of what was going on. I could see a few guys around two women while I was walking. I recognized that it was Sarah and Naomi that were surrounded. One of the guys pushed Sarah to the ground, and another one grabbed Naomi. When I caught a glimpse of that, I completely lost it. I rushed over and hit the dude that had pushed her down. I then hit the other two guys and knocked them on the ground as well. By this time, Naomi had gotten away and had gone to get help. I had a choice; let them get up and go three on one with them, or keep them down until help came or until they ran off. I chose to go on the offensive and went after the guy that laid his hands on Sarah. I caught him with a knee to the face, pounced on top of him and pounded his ass a few more times; all the while also keeping an eye on the other two that were still laying on the ground. Then, from out of nowhere, a fourth person appeared; striking me in the back of the head with a hard object. I fell to the ground and landed on my left shoulder, with my right arm being exposed. My first thought once I was hit was to protect my arm from getting injured; I think I attempted to do that. This was the last thing I remember before I blacked out.

When I regained consciousness, it was sometime the next morning and I was laying in a hospital. I had bruises all over my body, my right arm was twice the size of my left, and I had a killer headache. The doctor informed me that I had a concussion, and my shoulder and elbow would require surgery. He notified me the surgery would happen a few days after the swelling had gone down. The police were there to ask me a few questions about what had happened. They told me that according to eyewitnesses; one guy, assumed to be in his early twenties, struck me in the back of the head with a wood bat and he hit me numerous times to the body, mainly to the arm. They believed the four people were college students and probably in town for the concert on Saturday night. There was not anyone that could positively identify the four men and according to the police, the eyewitnesses were too far away to get a good look at the four guys. I was not too happy when I heard that; I knew someone saw something! The officers told me that they were sorry that they could not do more to find the ones responsible, and wished me the best of luck in the future.

       I was really pissed off! I got my ass kicked by some college punks; because I was defending a girl that I would probably never see again. It would be a long time before I could pitch again and I missed the Mplants concert. The band had given me back stage passes and everything. What a great night! I called my parents and told them what had happened. Of course, they were concerned and wanted to come to Jacksonville. I told them that there was nothing they could do until after my surgery; then I would go home to California and see them. I was bored in the hospital; they did not have any movie channels, and I was unable to play any video games because of my injuries. It really killed me not being able to play Playstation. However, I did make the news, because of my good deed. I received many letters, cards, flowers, and balloons, but nothing from Sarah or her friend.

Chapter 2
Mr. Cummings

The doctor released me from the hospital on Monday morning and scheduled a check-up for later in the week. I was extremely happy to be leaving that place; I was bored and I had been feeling totally helpless since I was admitted. I was wheeled out of Jacksonville Memorial; bruised ego and all. Yet, I was optimistic that everything would eventually be okay. However, the cute nurse, who escorted me out, made me realize that it may not come as soon as I would like; when she told me that she doesn't go out with patients, not even "brave ones." Yeah, I think she had to have a boyfriend. Once we made it to the car, which the team had sent to take me home; I thanked her for taking excellent care of me. Finally, my hospital stay was over and I couldn't wait to get home.

On the way there, I noticed that we were going in the opposite direction of my apartment complex. The driver told me that the owner of the team wanted to see me first. We pulled up to an enormous house that had a long driveway and a huge yard, with the ocean in the background. There was a huge marble fountain in the middle of the circle driveway that immediately grabbed my attention; it was truly magnificent. I was instantly impressed with Mr. Cummings even before I saw the inside of his huge mansion. The front yard was wonderful; the monthly landscaping bill had to be insane. I slowly got out of the car, cautiously, trying not to bump my arm that was in a sling; then, proceeded toward the front door. There was a man, who looked in his early forties, at the door waiting to greet me; he was not Mr. Cummings.

"Kastle Raines, it is a pleasure to meet you. I'm Banks, a die hard Suns' fan and a huge fan of yours. I was at the game on Friday and you were simply amazing. I have never seen a perfect game before. The ump was completely wrong; without question it was definitely a strike." He said this with a huge smile on his face, while he gave me a stern handshake.

"Thank you! I thought so too," I quickly concurred.

"I hated to hear about your accident; that was unfortunate. I am truly sorry." He sounded almost as devastated as I was. He opened the door for us and we walked in the house.

"It was just an unfortunate incident that I wish I could change the outcome; but, for that particular girl, I would do it all over again," I said. We continued to walk and talk a while, as I followed him through the house.

"Was that your girlfriend that you came to the rescue of?"

"No, I met her that night. It may sound crazy, but in that short time I felt something very special for her. There was no way that I was going to stand by and let anything happened to her; no matter what it cost me. At that moment, I didn't think at all; I just reacted," I truthfully stated to the man that I had just met.

"It sounds like it was love at first sight," he replied.

"I thought so, but I haven't heard anything from her. I lost her number and she is unlisted. The way my week is going, I am pretty sure that I will never see her again!" I said, as we reached the door that lead to the backyard.

"I am sorry for your misfortune. I hope everything works out for you," he sincerely replied, as he escorted me to the table on the back patio. It was beside an outdoor bar that, had stools all around it. Also nearby was an extravagant spa that spilled over into an Infiniti Pool; located by a rather spacious pool house that immediately got my attention.

"Thank you," I said, while I continued checking out the surroundings.

"Here… have a seat. There is someone who is anxious to see you. There's some breakfast here; please help yourself to anything you want. I have to go inside; here is some interesting reading material you may like to read. " The man said, as he sat me down at the table that had a huge breakfast spread on it; and handed me a newspaper before he walked away.

"Thank you! Everything looks great," I replied when he was walking away. I began to wonder what Mr. Cummings was going to say to me. I thought to myself that this guy was being way too nice. I'm about to be let go from the team, even before I can see if I can come back from the injuries. I then began to notice something strange. I looked down at the plate in front of me, and there was already a ham and cheese omelet on it. I always had that for breakfast. There also was a glass of orange juice and cup of coffee that I took a sip of. The coffee was a gourmet blend that had cream and sugar in it, just the way I like it. I thought that was weird. I wondered how in the hell the owner of my team knew so much about me. After I finished off the omelet, I began to read the paper while drinking my coffee. I came across a very interesting story in the newspaper; when, suddenly, I felt someone tapping on my shoulder. I turned around and immediately I was met with a kiss. I caught a glimpse of a woman with long dark hair in the split second I had when I turned around; but I couldn't make out the face. I opened my eyes after a few seconds to identify who was kissing me. It was Sarah!

"Hey there!" I said, absolutely shocked to see her.

"That was nice," she replied while her lips were still only inches away from my face.

"Yes, it was! This is a total surprise; I thought I would never see you again," I responded. I went back in for another kiss.

"I'm sorry that I didn't visit you, but I haven't been in a hospital since my mom died. Although, I was on my way until my dad said that he wanted to talk to you and he would have you brought here."

"Well, I'm glad to see you. I can't believe that you didn't mention that Mr. Cummings is your father," I said. I was in shock that, Sarah, this beautiful woman, was the owner's daughter.

"No, I don't know who that is," she replied, with a confused look on her face.

"Then where are we?" I asked.

"This is my father's house; what, he didn't tell you?"

"No, the driver told me that the owner of the Suns wanted to see me. I thought your father worked for him." I assumed Banks was the butler or something like that; I didn't think he looked like a butler, but what does a butler suppose to look like. I then suddenly heard a familiar voice coming from behind me.

"My name is Banks Newman; it is a pleasure to finally meet you," he said, as he appeared in eye view; eventually, stopping in front of the table.

"Well, I'm going to go change and give you two an opportunity to talk," Sarah said, as she put her arm around me and kissed me on the forehead before she went into the house.

"Mr. Newman, the breakfast was great. Thank you."

"You are welcome; but, please, call me Banks," he replied, as he sat down in the chair across from me.

"I like that. Where did it come from?" I asked.

"My name is Roosevelt Baines Newman. I was named after Franklin D. Roosevelt and Lyndon Baines Johnson. When I was young my parents called me R.B., my friends later gave me the name Banks. I really don't remember exactly how it came about. Some kid came up with it and it just stuck, over the years. Did you see anything interesting in the there?" he asked, as he pointed at the newspaper that was lying on the table.

"Yeah, there's an article here that gives me chills; it brings back some bad memories," I responded.

"How so?" Banks asked.

"When I was seven, I was hospitalized for being stung by a large number of hornets. It was definitely the worst experience of my childhood and something I will never forget." I read an article in the newspaper that stated four college students from Gainesville were found Sunday morning with their hands, feet, mouth, and eyes ducked taped. They had been piled on top of each other with no clothes on, inside of a phone booth that was located near the college. Each of the students had their hair painted pink, and had been stung many times from a hornets nest that was inside the phone booth. The students said they were placed there by men in ski masks; the local police believed it to be a fraternity prank.

"What do you think about the story?" Banks asked.

"I feel for anyone who is stung by hornets," I answered, with the utmost sympathy for the hornets' victims.

"Those pieces of shit deserved worse; they should be six feet deep for touching my daughter. They are lucky!" Banks said with rage in his voice. I was completely stunned with his statement.

"These four mother fuckers did this to me?" I inquired angrily, as I pointed at the newspaper.

"Yes, it was them. Those pricks don't have any respect and their careless actions warranted some form of retribution," Banks answered.

"Well, maybe they will think twice before they ruin someone else's life," I said. Then, I took a bite of the ham and cheese omelet that was on the plate in front of me.

"I believe everything happens for a reason; and from what I've seen Kastle, you are going to be okay," Banks responded.

"All of this is impressive; my favorite breakfast, the four attackers, and my bad experience with hornets. How in the hell do you know all of this?" I asked.

"I know all! If there is anything that you ever need, just let me know!" Banks mysteriously replied. "I'm sorry that I have to run off, but I have a business meeting to go to; just make yourself at home. It was really great to meet you. Please, don't be a stranger," he said. Then he shook my hand again and walked back in to his house. A few minutes later, Sarah joined me on the patio. She set an Mplants t-shirt on the table and sat down in the chair to the right of me.

"I felt bad about going to the concert when you couldn't, but Naomi forced me to go. However, once I bought you a souvenir I felt a little less guilty," she said. She had a good explanation for her actions, even though it was unnecessary.

"You shouldn't feel guilty at all. It was just a freak accident; it happens. It will be okay. I'll have the surgery and I'll be back good as new," I assured her.

"I know you wanted to go to the concert Saturday; so, the least I can do is to take you to their next concert in Miami," she said, as I took a sip of my coffee.

"I would love to go to Miami with you; thank you. I'm going to have a lot of free time next week and over the next couple of months. When do we leave?" I asked.

"It's not until next Saturday," Sarah said, as she grabbed a few grapes from a fruit tray that was in the center of the table.

"That will work out great. I have to see the doctor on Thursday to schedule my surgery; then I will be free for the weekend."

"It should be fun. My dad will fly us there on his private jet and we can make a weekend out of it," Sarah replied.

"Definitely! So what does your father do? He has an enormous house, a private jet, and a nice selection of toys in the driveway; he's living large."

"My father was in the Army for ten years. Afterwards, he started his own security business and has done quite well for himself from various investments he made. I try to stay out of his business, so that is about all I know. The only business he has now is a security company; RB Security."

"So he has a security guard business?" I asked.

"No, it's a body guard business. They protect famous people and really anyone who pays for their services. They get paid very well," Sarah said, while she was eating her grapes.

"That's cool. It looks like business is good," I replied. We continued talking and enjoying our breakfast.

From that day forward, Sarah and I were together all the time. If we were not at her apartment, then we were at mine. We went to the concert the next weekend and had a great time. We flew to Miami in her father's private jet, which is definitely the way to travel. I wanted one! Furthermore, I wanted what it symbolized; success! Up to that point in my life, I had relied on my right arm for any success that I might have.

A few days later, I had the surgery on my arm. Afterwards, the doctor informed me that it would be at least a year before I could start pitching again and that was only if the rehab went as planned. He also said that my arm would never be the same, which was difficult to handle. The team dropped me from the roster, but offered me a job as a pitching coach. They told me I would have a job with the team when I was ready to come back. I was truly devastated. My dream since I was a child was officially crushed at that moment. Sarah was there for me; she told me that I would rehab and come back better than ever, but I was realistic and I knew my baseball career was over.

Everyday after receiving the crushing diagnosis, there was a popular phrase that crossed my mind: "what the hell will I do now?" I wanted to be rich and successful. I knew a job as a coach in the minor leagues would not buy me a private jet and was not what I wanted to do.

I continued to rehab my arm for months. I was around Sarah and her father all of the time. Banks Newman was successful; so, when he talked, I listened. I thought if I listened to him, I would come up with some sort of a plan for the future or at least the next step.

Chapter 3
The Next Episode

One day, a few weeks later, Banks asked me about my plans for the future. He told wanted me to work for him. He said that he only hires people that he trusts and he could see me, eventually, running the business. I took that as if he was saying that I was part of the family. I took him up on his offer and began learning about the business. He had me do all the deskwork until I was healthy enough to start training for the fieldwork. In fieldwork, we provided our clients with protection all over the world. Most of our clients were famous movie stars and sports stars; there were a few government officials that we provided security for during their vacations and other occasions. Banks charged a lot for our services; but, he trained each employee himself to ensure that each one met his standards. He made sure everyone knew what to do in every situation. He trained them in protecting themselves and the client at all costs. Banks' employees were well skilled in every aspect of the job, once the training period was concluded.

I was in charge of assigning our clients with security personnel. After a while, I began to get many new clients. I used my selling skills, that I did not know I had, along with smooth talking to fill the calendar with assignments. Business was so good that Banks needed to hire more staff. I presented Banks with the new and improved assignment calendar; he was very impressed, to say the least. I informed him that no one would have a day off for three months without more personnel. I had a few questions for Banks about what I thought could be causing the staffing problems. I was curious about the four names I saw on the payroll roster that were not on the personnel list I had. If they were on the schedule, I figured it would be easier on everyone. He told me that he had assigned them a job for the entire year; therefore, I had to think of a new problem solving solution. He began looking over the "new client list" and was thrilled when he saw the name Tristan Lake.

"How in the hell did you get Tristan?" Banks asked.

"The biggest movie star in the world should be protected by the best security staff. He wasn't too happy with his only encounter with RB Security. It took me a while to get him, but as long as I vouched for the person we send, he was all for it. What can I say, he likes me?"

"Well I guess we need to get you trained then. He will be your first assignment," Banks stated. Obviously, I was excited to hear that. I was finally getting out of the office and I was definitely looking forward to getting started on training.

I began my training a few days later; Banks moved me into his house for the duration of the process. We got started every morning at five o'clock; running five miles and then swimming numerous laps in the pool, or vice versa. Then, I would hit the heavy bag and speed bag for 30 minutes. We would then spar for another 30 minutes and we would repeat that cycle until lunchtime. After lunch, we would go to the gun range that he had on his property to practice my shooting skills with a variety of weapons. Before the gun range, the only experience I had with shooting was with paintball guns and first person video games. However, it did not take long for me to get the hang of the real thing. We would then workout with weights for about two hours before our cycle of running, hitting the bags, and sparring.

Every night we would go to a restaurant and a bar. We did not go to party; my training would not allow it. However, we always had fun; which was a prerequisite for Banks. He always said, "Everyone should enjoy himself or herself every second of every day." He wanted me to have fun with this job, but always be in control of every situation. During this training period, he would prepare me for the situations that I would encounter on the job. Banks demanded that all of his employees wear nice suits and be in great shape. He instructed me to train myself to notice everything. From the time I walk into a room until I leave it; each person and every object. "Attention to detail" was something he stressed in every exercise or scenario we went through; he said those three words countless times. He wanted me to always be courteous and respectful, "treat the client like a king," he said; but, never take any shit from anyone. He told me to carry a Zippo, a pack of cigarettes, a pack of gum, a cell phone, and sunglasses. If I needed to get information from a person; I was to offer them a piece of gum, or a cigarette, or light a cigarette to start the conversation. He said they would feel like that they had to talk to me; which did make sense. There was one thing that he told me I should do. Client or not, always light a woman's cigarette. Wear sunglasses so you can look at everything without anyone noticing. In addition, a cell phone carried at all times, with all-important numbers programmed in the phone. The client's safety always comes first in every situation. Therefore, I learned CPR, and the correct way to use a fire extinguisher; along with a number of other safety procedures.

In my spare time, I would listen to tapes to teach myself a few different foreign languages; even though Banks did not require that; he was impressed that I took the initiative. I learned some words, but I am far from fluent in any language other than English. Banks wanted to know everything, especially what was being said around him and he wanted his people to be the same way.

Banks wanted to know about my experiences and everything that I had done in my life. My life was centered on my baseball career, so I hardly ever did anything else. He wanted me to have experiences with everything imaginable. We would train during the week, and do stuff I have never done before on the weekends. I have never had as much fun in a six week period, Sarah went with us on these trips and we began to get closer and closer. One weekend we would go snow skiing and deep-sea fishing and sailing the next. We also went sky diving, bungee jumping, water skiing, and deep-sea diving; all of it was totally awesome.

Another skill that I had to master was to be able to drive anything that moved. Banks gave me lessons on flying a plane, a helicopter, a speed boat, and set it up for me to learn to operate a train. I had to be able to drive at fast speeds, so I would do 50 laps twice a week in a stock car at the local track. I also took a high-speed driving class at the police academy. They had an obstacle course that was very realistic; now that was fun to do. I learned to ride a motorbike too; it wasn't hard to do, but I was always cautious about not getting injured before. I was worried about my baseball career, so I did not do anything to jeopardize that. I loved riding! I loved it so much; the first day I rode a bike I had to have one. I bought one of my own, but I am still a little cautious. I do wear a helmet whenever I have a chance to ride.

One Sunday, toward the end of training, Banks and I went and played golf; we would go to the country club and play 18 holes every Sunday afternoon. Banks would usually take this time to go over situations and guidelines of being the best bodyguard that I could be. However, this round of golf was different. All he talked about was Sarah, while we both had the best round of golf that we ever played. We both shot a 72, which was by far our best scores on our Sunday golf outings.

"You know this is the happiest I have ever seen my daughter. You two are great together! I've seen how wonderful you treat her and I deeply thank you for that. I have really gotten to know you over the last few months, and I think the world of you; I think of you like a son." Banks said this with such conviction in his voice.

"I appreciate that; it means a lot to me. I hope you know, I think a lot of you too. I've had a hard time adjusting these past few months, but thanks to you and Sarah, everything is great," I replied. This is how he started the conversation about the rule regarding having sex with clients.

"I have a rule that I tell all of my employees; no sex with a client during a job. After the job, I don't care. In your case, sex with a client is not an option. Sarah is still my little girl; I know she does it, but I don't like to talk about it and I really don't like thinking about it. If you're on a job for an extended period of time, I have a G4 on standby that will bring her to wherever you are," Banks said with a serious look on his face. That's the way

Banks was; he made sure that you knew when he was serious about something.

"Banks, you have nothing to worry about. I will follow all of your rules, especially that one. In fact, if I wasn't so cautious; I would probably be asking for your blessing," I replied.

"If I wasn't so cautious, I would be giving my blessing; just give it some time. You'll know when the time is right," Banks said with a hint of fatherly happiness. I thought it was funny that when Banks brought up sex, the conversation turned to marriage; he could be a little intimidating at times. When we got off that uncomfortable subject, he informed me that my training was almost over and I would be providing personal security to clients in the upcoming week.

The first one was the Mayor's wife; her husband and Banks were good friends. She really did not need a body guard; she only took on trainees as a favor to Banks. However, as I later found out; she does enjoy the personal attention. I arrived at her house at around 9:00 A.M. I walked to the door and when it opened, I was totally surprised at what happened next.

"Whoa, you're Kastle Raines!" A woman said with a sexy grin.

"I am and you are Mrs. Sterling?" I asked, while I stood in front of the doorway.

"Please, call me Cindy. Please come in! Can I get you anything to drink; a protein shake perhaps?" She asked, as I followed behind her.

"Sure. That will be great," I answered as we walked in to the kitchen and she began making our drinks with her blender.

"I always have one before my Pilates class. You know, Banks didn't tell me who he was sending over, but I have to say, he really did good this time," she said before she started the blender. She was a very attractive woman in her early forties, and she looked to be in very good shape. Mrs. Sterling was already dressed for her class. She was wearing a sports bra and spandex pants that showed off her hot body. At that point, I knew this job was going to be hard. I was a one-woman man and that was not going to change; I just had to concentrate on my job and protect my client.

"Here you go Mr. Raines," she said, as she handed me a glass filled with protein shake that I gladly accepted.

"Thank you."

"You are so welcome," she said, as she was noticeably staring into my eyes. I took a sip of the shake and she did as well.

"So how did you know who I was, if Banks didn't tell you?" I asked.

"My husband is a huge baseball fan. I remember you from the ballgames I have been to in the past. Hey, wait here. I'll be right back," she said, as she walked out of the room. She returned a minute later with a baseball. "Will you sign this for me?" She asked.

"Sure, so you like baseball huh?" I replied, as I took the ball from her hand and, gladly, signed it for her.

"Not really, I go with my husband to games sometimes; but, it's not one of my favorite activities," she answered.

"Well, I'm flattered that you remembered me," I replied, as I took another sip of the protein shake.

"Oh, I remember you; if it wasn't for you, my husband would still try to get me to go to baseball games."

"Oh, is it because I don't play anymore?" I said.

"No. We went to a game over a year ago, and my husband wouldn't shut up about how great you were going to be in the big show; that's all he talked about before, during, and after the game. I didn't know what he was talking about; I just thought you were cute. On our ride home after the game he finally stopped talking about baseball and started talking about sex. Sports, sex, and politics are all the man thinks about. He had read an article about the top five famous people on married couples's sex list. He brought up the idea for us to make a list and I agreed, I even let him make the guidelines. He made his top eight list and then I made mine," Mrs. Sterling explained. She now had my full attention after the topic of sex was brought up.

"Why eight? Why not a top five or top ten?" I said trying to seem interested in her story, even though the conversation was getting a little uncomfortable.

"He couldn't decide on only five, so I gave him eight. Who knew a year and a half after we made our lists, number 2 on mine would be standing in my kitchen," She said, as I let out a quiet chuckle, after hearing the surprising statement. I couldn't believe that I was on her celeb list, but what was more astonishing that I was number 2.

"What? No way!" I replied.

"It's true," she responded reassuringly.

"Who was number 1 on your list?" I asked.

"Tristan Lake," she replied with somewhat of a dreamy smile on her face.

"Now he is famous. I on the other hand, am not. It's hard to believe that I am number 2 on your celeb list."

"When the list was made, you were famous to my husband. I put you at number 2 because you're cute. Plus, I never had to go to another game, again."

"Do you have the list in writing or a laminated card; something I can look at to verify this?" I asked.

"Relax sexy, we don't have to do anything. I have a signed baseball now. My husband will never believe that we didn't have sex. I'm ready to go to my class now. Make sure you take good care of me today," she said, as she grabbed her bag and I escorted her to the car; all the while, feeling a little worried about her previous comments. We left her house, where I accompanied her to her Pilates class. When her class was over she showered and changed in the locker room, while I was waiting out front. When she met me in the front lobby, she had something to tell me.

"There is no list. Banks was testing you and you passed with flying colors. Now can you loosen up; I hope you're not mad at me. Nevertheless, if I did have a celeb list, you would certainly be on it," She confessed.

"I am relieved. Thank you for not dragging this out all day," I responded. We then left the gym and continued with the day.

Afterwards, we went to her daughter's school for a meeting she had with the principal. Sarah worked there, so I stopped by to say hello while I was there. She taught the second grade and she absolutely loved it. I could tell that she enjoyed it from her work conversations; but, once I saw her in action, I knew that she would be a teacher for life. Sarah was in the middle of an English lesson, so I did not stay long. I returned to the Principal's office and waited for my client outside the door. After her meeting, I took Mrs. Sterling to a restaurant, where she had lunch with a few of her friends. After she finished her meal and chatted with the ladies, I drove her back to her home; this finally brought the day to a close. Overall, it was a rather easy day; everything job related went exceptionally smooth.

The next day, I went to meet Banks at the gym where he was playing racquetball, to get my schedule for the day. I arrived there early, so I watched them play for a little while. Banks always said, "If you are not 15 minutes early, then you are late."

When their game was over, something the other guy did caught my attention. He turned his back to Banks, took off his wristband, and quickly put on his watch. The Omega Sea master he put on was almost exactly like the one I was wearing; except the dial color of his watch was black instead of blue. The watch first got my attention, but then I noticed that on his wrist was a tribal tattoo with the letter B and the number 5 in the middle of it, outlined by a watch tan line. The guy picked up his bag and went in to the locker room as Banks walked over to me.

"Do you want a shot at me now?" Banks said, as he stood in front of me with his racquet still in his hand.

"I ain't scared, but maybe another day. I'm ready to go to work."

"Good answer. I'm on fire today," Banks responded, as he sat down and began to put his racquet in his bag.

"Who was the other guy?" I asked.

"That's Adam Marshall. He's a good friend of mine. We play at least once a week; even though I kick his ass every time."

"Are you sure he doesn't throw games?" I asked Banks.

"That's funny, no he is just as competitive as I am; I'm just better. He has beaten me before, well maybe once."

"I think I will take you up on that offer. I'll play you," I said. Saying this, only to see what his response would be.

"Maybe another time; you are late for work and you have a busy day ahead of you. There's a client waiting for you as we speak. Today you will be providing security for a local author, Colby Phelps. Tonight you will be accompanying my beautiful daughter, as her personal bodyguard, to a night out on the town. I can't have her mad at me and apparently I've been keeping you busy with your training. This way you can spend time with each other and train; keeping everybody happy. I have rented a limo that will take you and Colby to a book signing that he has at Jack's Book Cave. It should be here in a few minutes," Banks said.

"Okay, I will take care of it. They are both in good hands," I replied.

"We'll see about that. I've instructed them to send report cards upon completion," Banks responded. I walked outside and caught my ride in the limo that Banks had arranged for the day.

We arrived at Colby Phelps' home, which was about fifteen minutes from the gym. Colby approached the limo, as soon as we pulled up. He was humbled and immediately grateful for Banks's gesture. He was not a famous author; in fact, this was his first book. Banks first met him at a coffee shop downtown, while Colby was there writing his book. They saw each other regularly ultimately; he sold Banks his first book. Banks was so impressed that, he sent me as a gift for the launch of his new book. Banks was like that, if he liked you he would do anything for you. I quickly realized that Banks was a good person to know. Take this guy for example; he may or may not ever be a best selling author, but on that day his hard work was rewarded by Banks.

When we arrived at Jack's Book Cave, there were only five people there waiting for him; and they were family and friends. However, sometimes it helps if you look important even if no one knows who you are. With a limo parked outside, a personal bodyguard by his side, the line of people went from five to one hundred. In the five hours we were there, he signed over three hundred books. Afterwards, Colby was a happy man and very grateful for me being there. The hours I spent with him were really humbling; it was a privilege to witness a person's goal being achieved. My day with Colby came to a close as we returned to his home; ending a truly satisfying experience for the both of us.

Later that night, Sarah and I went to Club Diamond. It was the first time we had been there since the first night we met. I was happy to be there spending time with Sarah; it was nothing like my previous gig. I was there to do a job, but it was more like a date. I paid for everything, normally a bodyguard does not do that for his client; in fact she did not bother to bring anything with her in the club. It did not bother me at all; I would not have it any other way. It was really a nice, relaxing night out with my beautiful girlfriend.

We stayed there just an hour or two and then began to head home; it had been a long day, and I was definitely ready to get my girlfriend all tucked in to her bed. As we were walking through the parking lot, there were a few vehicles beginning to leave the parking area. There were two cars, then a van passing by us. From the first day I met Banks, I listened to everything he said, and tried to use everything he had taught me. In the past few weeks, I had been training myself to notice everything and keep my brain working at all times. Therefore, the black cargo van in the parking lot, surrounded by a number of luxury cars and sports cars, immediately raised a red flag. When we finally reached our car, the two cars had already exited the parking lot. That was the moment that I received a text message on my phone. I looked down to see that the text was from Sarah. It read, "I love you." As soon as I saw it; I heard a sliding door open behind us.

"Kastle, watch out!" Sarah shouted from the other side of the car. As I started to turn around, I caught a glimpse of guys coming at us dressed in all black. Before I was able to turn completely around, someone grabbed me from behind. I, quickly, grabbed his arm, turning my body, flipping him over my shoulder. When he went to the ground, his sleeve came up, showing his white tattooed wrist. My first instinct was to help Sarah; instead I began to kick the masked man's ass. I kicked him hard in the ribs and then got on top of him and started whaling on him. I got in six or seven good licks before I was grabbed from behind. A rag soaked with chloroform was placed over my face and then I was stuffed in the van.

When I woke up, I was sitting in a chair handcuffed with my arms behind me. I was sitting at a table with only one more chair placed directly across from me. The room was small and empty with no windows, but there was a lot of light in there. When I looked around some more, I saw why. There was a video camera at the top of the wall directly facing me. After thoroughly scanning the room, the door opened. A black man, wearing a black mask, walked in and sat down in the chair across from me.

"You were in the wrong place at the wrong time; all we wanted was the girl. When we receive the ransom, you will be set free. As long as we get the money, you have my word no one will be harmed."

I waited a good ten seconds before I said anything to him. "Do you and your boys not like Adam, or did he think he was such a bad ass that he tried to take me by himself?" I said which produced a puzzled look on the face of the guy who was in the room with me.

"I don't know an Adam," the man quickly replied.

"Is there any way that I could have a cigarette? I am really dying for one. You can tell your boy with the tribal tattoo that has B5 in the middle of it, to bring it to me. It may or may not be his name; but for now, we'll call him Adam Marshall," I said.

"If I can find one, I will bring it to you," he said, as he got up from the table; noticeably glancing at the camera before he left the room. He exited with a smirk on his face.

After a few minutes had past, Adam walked in the room with a pack of cigarettes and a lighter. He sets the pack and the lighter on the table and then moves away. He leans back on the wall, crossing his arms, staring down at me.

"Who was that who was in here before? I like him; he seems like a real cool guy. I want to know his name, since I already know yours... Adam," I said which immediately forced a surprised reaction by Adam.

"Since you will never see any of us again; that includes Eve, I will tell you his name. His name is Dante Jackson," he replied with a pissed off look on his face.

"Who the hell is Eve?" I curiously asked him.

"Eve is the girl that you were with tonight; you know the hostage you let us take. Actually, she is not really a hostage; this whole thing was her idea. We're going take the money we get and get the hell away from her father. Eve is her middle name; I guess you two weren't as close as you thought. Adam and Eve, doesn't that sound good?" Adam said with a huge smile. Instead of gritting my teeth and losing my cool, I used my time wisely. There was nothing I could do about Sarah. She had made her choice, even though it was a dumb one.

"Yeah!" I replied. "You two will live happily ever after. How about that cigarette now? I could really use one."

"My sweetheart told me to give you anything you want and I will do anything for my baby," he responded; while he maintained a nonstop grin that made me more livid with every second that passed. After his comments, I just wanted to smack him.

"Great! She's a lucky gal," I said with a straight face. I could not bring myself to hide the fact that I was more than a little bothered with the information I was receiving from that whack job.

"Let me get you that cigarette. It looks like you need it." Looking like a grinning idiot, he approached the table leaning down to get the pack of cigarettes. I met him halfway, as I jumped out of the chair, over the table forcing him to the floor. This time when I got a hold of him, I drew blood. I pounded his face as much as I could before his boys pulled me off. They grabbed me and held me in a corner. When I finally began to calm down, I saw someone out of the corner of my eye in the doorway, it was Banks. He walked in the room and started giving orders.

"Everybody calm down! Kastle, everything is okay. Rocco and Mason take Adam to the hospital and stay with him. Also, make sure his ass is at my house tomorrow. Dante, sit Kastle down and light him a cigarette. Kastle, we have you a beer on the way."

They took Adam out of the room and I sat down at the table. Sarah, cautiously, stuck her head through the doorway to see if it was safe to enter. She walked over to me, handed me a beer, and apologized for her part in the night's events. "You have graduated; your training is finally over!" She explained the situation with a smile on her face.

"Thank God! Look, I'm sorry I sent him to the hospital; but he just went too far, he really had me going. I had to do something. I couldn't just sit there and take all of the things he was saying. Plus, I thought he had crossed you. I had to get him," I forcefully said.

Banks stood in front of me with a look of satisfaction on his face. "I'm impressed! How did you get the cuffs off? I watched you the whole time; I didn't see you do it."

"I've tried to be prepared for every situation; so I learned a few things you haven't taught me," I replied.

"So, it was the tattoo that gave him up; I didn't know he even had one," Banks said with a satisfying grin, as he rehashed the incident that had just taken place.

"Yeah, I saw it when you were playing racquetball. What does B5 stand for?" I said to the guys.

"That is what Marshall calls us. B5... it stands for Banks' five," Dante answered.

"You've had enough excitement for one night; go home and I'll see you tomorrow. Come by the house tomorrow afternoon at two o'clock. We have something to talk about," Banks said as Sarah and I headed to her house for the night; and she drove. I still had the adrenaline pumping and she did not think I would drive safely. On the way to her house, Sarah had a lot that she wanted to tell me.

"It is a big mystery what my dad, Adam, and the other guys do; they are always around each other. I don't know if it's illegal or not and I don't want to know, but I do have eyes. He has always kept me away from it. In the past, if I asked a question about his business, he was always extremely vague with his answer. After tonight, he is going to ask you to join Adam and the other guys to do whatever they do. I just wanted to prepare you. I was standing right next to him as we watched you impress all of us. You were just like my father tonight; always on top of things. You had a swagger and a determination about you that I haven't seen before. I really don't know what he has in store for you; that will be for you two to decide. After seeing you in action, I'm not worried anymore. I'm behind you one hundred percent in whatever you decide to do. I love you so much."

"I love you too. I'm happy to hear that; this gives me something to think about. I'll talk to him and see what he has planned for me," I replied, as I held her hand.

"I want to tell you something. It is nothing big; I just want you to know everything about me," Sarah said, with a slightly different tone in her voice. That tone had me, momentarily, wondering what she was about to tell me.

"Okay; I want to know everything about you," I responded, very interested in the upcoming conversation.

"My parents adopted me when I was a baby; but, they're the only family I have ever known. I don't know who my birth parents are and I have never cared to find out. I have had a wonderful life; I was so lucky that my parents found me. After my mom died in a car accident when I was twelve, it has been just my dad and me ever since. I have a great life that he has given me and I love him dearly," Sarah said, as I held her free hand.

"I'm sorry you had to go through that tragedy. I want only happiness for you now and in the future."

"That is enough about that, let's talk about something else. You know you were really great tonight. It was the first time I've ever been involved in anything like that. I am really turned on."

"I am too, Eve." I said sarcastically, along with big smile.

"I'm so sorry about that. Yes, Eve is my middle name. Adam has had a crush on me for a long time, but I never was interested in him. He is a real jerk and he has always creeped me out. We have never gone out and never will," Sarah responded.

"I believe you, baby. I was just kidding. I am okay now. We've had a long night; it feels so good to be home," I said, as we arrived at home. Without question, we both were eager to get there. The sex we had that night was off the charts.

Chapter 4
I got my Button

The next afternoon Sarah and I rolled out of bed and went to her father's house. We did not get much sleep the night before; it was simply a great night. Even though we slept in later than usual, we still made it there on time. Banks wanted us there early before the others showed up so he and I would have a chance to talk. When we arrived, Banks was waiting for us by the pool.

"Kastle, have a seat and let me get you something to drink. Sweetheart, give us a few minutes to chat," he said, as he walked behind the fully stocked bar. "What would you like to drink?" He asked, as he began to put ice in the glasses.

"Grey Goose and Red Bull, if you have it?" I asked. I really never had a particular drink. I always switched up, depending on what I had a taste for at that particular moment.

"Yeah, I have almost everything here. So you're trying something new, huh?" Banks said with a surprised look on his face.

"Yes, I can use some Red Bull right now," I replied as he handed me my drink. He had his usual bourbon on the rocks.

"You are going to be a great asset to my business; to what part, will be up to you. If you choose to be a bodyguard, we would be honored to have you. However, you would be gone a lot more than you and my daughter would like. You will be paid well and will earn an honest living being away from home sometimes months at a time. Instead, I want you to join my crew. I wouldn't ask you if I didn't think you could handle this. I think you are made for it. The jobs we do could be dangerous and sometimes somewhat illegal. My crew is like a well oiled machine; we are very good at what we do, the job is completed safely, and everyone always comes home. We make a ton of money and enjoy life to the fullest in the present, instead of waiting for the future. Nevertheless, if you decide you don't want to do this, I'll understand; and of course, everything that was said here doesn't go any further," Banks said, while he was drinking his bourbon.

"What kind of jobs would I be doing?" I asked, as I took a swallow of my drink.

"I trust you with my life; but if you're not in our circle, it is best that you don't know the details of the business. You will just have to trust me," Banks said.

I walked over to the bar, picked up two shot glasses, and filled them with Patron. I gave Banks one of the shots as I returned to my seat and sat down. "I'm sorry I let you go on so long. After last night, I decided that if you ever asked me to be one of your guys, like the four I met last night, I would say yes. I'm in. Here's to enjoying life to the fullest," I said, as we both raised our glasses.

"Outstanding! I am so happy to have you," Banks said with a smile.

"Cheers!" I said.

"I'll drink to that. Cheers!" Banks responded as we both took our shots. "What is this? I was expecting bourbon." He asked.

"Patron, it's good stuff!" I replied as put my shot glass on the table.

"It's not that bad, if you chase it with a shot of bourbon," Banks replied, as he took a sip of his bourbon.

"The other guys should be here soon, so everyone can get to know each other. Everything is going to be great," Banks said, as we had another shot while we were waiting.

When the others arrived, Banks brought us to the pool house to talk in private. The wives and girlfriends began to greet each other and get their drinks from the bar. Banks had the four of us sit at the table, while he stood in front of us with his drink in hand.

"I wanted everyone to hear this at the same time, so there will be no confusion. I know we are missing one, but I am going to go ahead and get this out of the way. I will fill Adam in when he gets here. Everyone, this is Kastle Raines. He will be joining our group. You four will be working together, Adam will be leading you. I will be in charge, but from afar. Adam will be a messenger for me and he will handle the business; however, all decisions will be made by me. I just need to take a step back and make more appearances at my company. Kastle has a security job in Miami that he has to complete before he joins us; so, it will be a little while before this is set into motion. Now, everyone come congratulate Kastle; make him feel a part of the team," Banks said.

"We'll make him feel like part of the family. Come here you! You're beautiful! Congratulations, you are now one of us; you're a made guy. You can call me Rocco; it is a pleasure to meet you," Rocco said.

"This is Roccolinni Brasace," Banks introduced him to me, as he shook my hand and gave me a peck on both cheeks. I did not want to show any disrespect, so I didn't pull away from the two-cheek kiss. It didn't bother me; I felt like it was just a peck, not a kiss. It was the first time I had a man kiss me on the cheek.

"Thank you," I said, giving him an appreciated nod.

"This is Mason Dunn," Banks said as the next guy walked up to us.

"Congratulations! I'm not into the Italian tradition of kissing; how about a handshake." However, I found out later that he is of Italian blood; he is part Italian American and part African American.

"Thank you," I told him, after letting out a short, but respectful laugh.

"And you know, this is Dante Jackson," Banks said as he formally introduced us.

"Congratulations! It is good to have you; I'm glad that we are on the same side now," Dante said, as he shook my hand.

"I appreciate your hospitality and I'm really excited to have the opportunity to be a part of this team," I said, after I had met everyone.

"Since the introductions are over with, I have a training video from the exercise last night for you guys to watch," Banks said, as he turned on the video.

"Is this what I think it is?" I asked, as the surveillance footage of Adam and I sitting at the table from the night before was beginning to play.

"Whoa!" Mason said, as the part where I first hit Adam was shown.

"Wow!" Dante yelled out, while the fight was still going on. Well, it was more like Adam taking hit after hit.

"I like it now, but at the time I didn't. We had to stay at the emergency room for two hours," Mason said.

"Yes! I love it. Please, I got to have a copy of this," Rocco replied when the surveillance video was over with.

"I'll see what I can do," Banks said as he turned off the television.

"Adam will probably destroy it, if he ever shows up," Mason replied.

"You guys have all night to bullshit and get to know each other. For now let's get back to the party; it's time to have a good time. Kastle and I will meet you out there," Banks said, as the other guys left the pool house.

"Is this where I should kiss your ring, your hand, or something?" I asked.

"That is what I wanted to talk to you about. Rocco loves his Italian traditions and mafia movies. This is not a gang or the mob. Nevertheless, we are a close group; we love and respect each other, and we make a lot of money. I just wanted to make sure that we were clear on everything. Now, let's go, we have a party to get to." Banks said, as we walked out of the pool house and continued toward the bar. On the way, Rocco stops me and he hands me a glass of wine; while Banks went on to the bar.

"Kastle, I have you something to drink. Here's to us. Salut!"

"Salut!" I said, as we both raised our glasses and then took a sip of Rocco's wine.

"How do you like the wine?" Rocco asked.

"I like it!" I replied

"I brought it for the Boss. It is a Super Tuscan wine I had sent from Italy; it's magnificent. Make sure your lady gets some too; 'in vino veritas,' wine is good for your relationship," Rocco said.

"What does that mean? Is that an Italian phrase?" I inquired.

"It is a Latin phrase that means 'in wine there is truth.'" Rocco answered.

"Do you give wine to your lady?" I asked Rocco, as I took another sip.

"My wife, yes; my goomah no. I don't want to hear anything from her," Rocco responded.

Dante walked over and stood by me and listened to our conversation, translating when necessary. "Goomah is his girl on the side; his mistress," Dante said to me.

Rocco then gets closer to me and puts his arm around my neck and began to talk to me in a softer tone. "I can't believe that cocksucker is going to be the consigliere. It felt so good to see you rough him up; I want to give Adam a beating at least three times a week. He busts my balls every fucking day; but my hands are tied, because he's a made guy and he can't be touched. That order can only come from the Boss."

I, immediately, looked at Dante and he then began to translate for me. "Marshall is now second in command. Banks doesn't allow any fighting in his crew; it is understood, it just doesn't happen. Therefore, no order from Banks will have to be given to have one of us clipped." I knew then, that I would have to go to my DVD collection and brush up on mafia lingo. I watch gangster movies all the time, but I still did not know some of the words that he was using.

"Dante is a team guy; but, he knows as well as I do, he loved seeing Adam get what he had coming to him," Rocco replied, as we smiled after his comments. I stood there with the guys and found myself sizing up each of them. Mason and Dante were about the same size; they are a little taller than I am, but not by much. They both are about six foot three inches tall, and around two hundred twenty pounds. I am six foot one inch and I stay around two hundred pounds. Rocco was a couple of inches shorter and a few pounds lighter than me. Banks was about the same size as Rocco; and Adam was about my size, but I was in better shape. Everyone was in good shape, including Banks; I hope I look that good when I am in my early forties.

"Kastle, I have always wanted to know how a pitcher can throw so hard. I have a strong arm, but I'm lucky if can get it up to 70 mph. What's the secret?" Dante asked.

"Chin ups," I replied.

"Are you serious?" Dante responded in disbelief.

"I swear! I did all the chin ups I can do, until I could not do anymore. I started on the monkey bars when I was five years old and I have done them everyday since then," I said.

"Bullshit... that's hard to believe," Dante replied.

"Hey, it worked for me," I responded.

"Yeah it works; but not with a fastball," Dante said.

"Trust me, it works." I said.

"What's the hardest that you have ever thrown? Have you ever hit 100 mph?" Dante asked.

"I threw 99 mph once. In fact, that was when I, first, hurt my arm. I was with a couple guys, playing around with the radar gun; we began to see who could throw the hardest. I tried over and over again to hit a hundred, but I couldn't; after that day, my arm never felt the same," I said.

"That sucks!" Dante replied.

"Yeah!" I replied and then changed the subject. "Look, I have to know about the frat boys that were stuffed in a phone booth. Banks hinted that he was involved, but he never confirmed it." I said to Rocco and Dante.

"Yes, it was us. The pricks needed to be scolded and we took care of them," Rocco responded.

"Who came up with the idea of the hornets?" I asked.

"It was Banks, but the phone booth was all us. Banks told us about your run in with hornets and he thought it was perfect under the circumstances. It is amazing what Banks and his sources can find out," Dante replied.

"Yes, it is; it's scary what they know," Rocco added.

"I want to thank all of you for not allowing those punks to get away with what they did," I responded.

"There had to be repercussions for their actions," Dante added.

"It was our pleasure. At the time we didn't know you, but Sarah is family and we take care of our own," Rocco replied.

"I would have loved to have been there," I said, with a smile on my face.

After a while, we were still standing by the pool; just talking and having a good time. From that point, I could tell I was going to enjoy working and hanging out with them. As Rocco would say, "I could tell that they were stand up guys." That is when it got interesting. Someone came up from behind me and started to push me in the pool. With my quick reflexes, I grabbed hold of his arm on the way in the pool. I saw it was Adam, so I let go. As I was falling I dowsed his white designer shirt with my glass of red wine before landing in the pool. It was a nice shirt; it was almost identical to mine. I got out of the pool, with my clothes now completely drenched; and, walked up to Adam, where the other guys were now gathered.

"Oh, I forgot that you are a surfer dude; you like the water," Adam said, as he had a look of satisfaction on his face. He was definitely proud of his actions.

"You were out of order! What was that, payback?" Rocco said to Adam, as he laughed at him.

"Do you feel better?" I asked Adam, as I stood in front of him, still dripping wet.

"Yes, but this is far from over cowboy. A dip in the pool is nothing compared to what you have coming. You are on my shit list superstar and I can't see the day that you ever get off of it," Adam replied, as I noticed something in his hand. A string tied to his middle finger on his right hand. It was a string to a yoyo; he was playing with it the entire time he was speaking. I had not even seen a yoyo in years; plus, I found it rather strange.

"If you would have been on time, you would have known that you have just put your hands on a made guy and under our code; yes, it is indeed over." Rocco enjoyed being the one to bring Adam any bad news.

"No, he can't be one of us! He's been around for five seconds. A lucky punch earns him a shot to work with us, no way." Adam said in complete disbelief. I couldn't help to stare at Adam's continuous use of the yoyo.

"I am a team player. I would be happy to spar with you, so I can show you a few things." I offered to Adam.

"You should really take him up on that. You have to be a little embarrassed," Rocco said as he looked at Adam.

"He hit me with some cheap shots; but, he won't do it again," Adam said

"What are you thinking? You already look fatigued from pushing Kastle in the pool," Rocco said.

"We can stand toe to toe, anytime you want, and spar; but, if you say the wrong thing the gloves will come off," I replied.

"We'll do it one day," Adam said as he smiled.

"Whoa, big fella, you might want to think about it a little longer before you start issuing any challenges. Your losing streak is getting longer and longer." Dante said.

"Kastle has owned your ass rather easily," Mason added.

"Just let me know. I'm looking forward to it," I responded.

"I am too," Adam replied, as he continued to grin and play with his yoyo.

"Rocco, I'm sorry about spilling the wine," I said to him as he just smiled. "You have good taste in shirts," I told Adam, as I admired his shirt. This finally caused him to lose his smile.

"I like the color. A little Italian flavoring makes everything better," Rocco added, as he admired Adam's shirt.

"Fuck you!" Adam said, glaring at Rocco.

"Do you believe this fucking guy? You have gotten your ass kicked twice in the last twenty four hours. Do you want to make it three?" Rocco replied.

"You have been bitched an awful lot lately," Mason said to Adam.

"Fuck off, Mason!" Adam replied.

"Yo, you should really take it easy; no one wants to go to the emergency room again," Dante added.

"You too? Believe me, if I go there, I'm bringing someone with me," Adam said to Dante with extreme confidence, as he finally stopped using the yoyo.

"Okay, why isn't anyone saying something about that? What is the deal?" I had to ask about the yoyo.

"We're used to it; that's his stress relief," Dante answered.

"He started using it a while back; after he went to an anger management class," Rocco explained to me.

"Come on; there's a ton of material with all of this," I replied.

"We have said it all, trust me. We don't even bother with any of it anymore; it is old news," Dante responded.

"You should be glad I have this or I would have cracked your head open, instead of pushing you in the pool," Adam said, as he opened his hand to display his useful toy.

"Hey, I was just curious. Whatever it takes to keep you safe; I am all for it," I responded, as I glanced at Adam's toy.

"You two are going to have to get along. I'll take responsibility for the rocky start. My training exercise didn't go as I had planned; so, I am sorry. You guys will be working together a lot, so this ends here; now, shake hands," Banks said, as he stepped in and gave me a towel.

I was willing to do what Banks wanted, so I put out my hand; but Adam slapped it away. "A real man shakes hands with his right hand," Adam said referring to my left hand attempted hand shake.

I then walked up to Rocco and Dante with a smile on my face, and shook their hands with my right hand. "I am selective to whom I extend my right hand." I wouldn't have left out Mason, but at the time he was hitting on a chic by the bar; and from where I was standing she looked extremely hot.

"Enough, this shit ends right now! Adam you come with me, I need to catch you up to speed on everything. Everyone else, as you were," Banks said, as they went into the pool house and talked.

"I bet Adam dusts off his needles tonight," Rocco said.

"What are you talking about?" I curiously asked.

"Marshall used to juice up until a couple of months ago," Dante answered.

"Yeah, Banks had to crack the whip to make him stop," Rocco said.

"You were a baseball player, did you ever do it?" Dante asked.

"No, I was tempted though." I answered, and told the honest to God truth. "How about you guys?" I asked.

"No, we never have. We are gym rats; but we work our asses off to look like this," Dante responded, explaining how they have their massive physiques.

"Here it comes. Rocco get ready to bow down to your under boss," Mason said, as he suddenly showed up from out of no where. This was the first time that I was around Mason. I do have to admit that he did make a good first impression with his funny one-liner, as well as the other guys in the brief time that we had been around each other. In my first impressions, all of the guys seemed close, but Mason and Rocco appeared closer than the rest. It looked like Dante was the same with everyone; no more or no less.

"Here you go, busting my balls! I'll respect the title, but I answer to Banks. You know that I'm respectful, but I don't have to like the messenger. Why are you two busting my balls, Kastle is the new guy?" Rocco replied.

"Adam is not around to get it," Dante responded.

"Fuck the both of you... sir mix a lot and black guy pea," Rocco said to Mason and Dante, as we all completely lost it.

"Classic!" I said to Rocco, as I put my arm around him.

"Go ahead and laugh it up; dead arm cottage," Rocco said, not leaving me out of the conversation. Although, I thought his shot at Mason and Dante was much better.

"Kastle! Who's the client in Miami?" Dante asked me, after he had finished laughing at Rocco's funny remarks.

"Tristan Lake," I answered.

"I thought he was done with the company," Dante replied.

"Our pansy-ass leader fucked that up!" Rocco commented.

"Who Banks?" I surprisingly said, in response to Rocco's statement.

"Fuck no; the newly appointed bitch boy messenger. Listen to this; he leaves the biggest movie star in the world, alone in a hotel lounge to go fuck the cleaning lady. When he was done, he didn't even clean up. He left a fucking used rubber on the guy's bed." We all laughed pretty hard at Rocco's story.

"Are you serious? Adam did that?" I asked, during all of the laughter.

"Yes, he fucked the housekeeper and left the rubber on Tristan Lake's bed. Now, that is funny; every time I hear it; I laugh harder and harder," Dante replied.

"Banks told Tristan that he fired the guy who worked with him on the last job," I informed the guys of what was said.

"He was mad at the time, but that is Banks' boy; Adam will never be fired," Mason replied.

"So he has tenure," I responded.

"It is more like Banks has an untrustworthy leach permanently attached to his ass," Rocco said, as we all laughed.

"You guys are great. I didn't know what to expect at first. Ex-military are always labeled as hardcore people that do not speak civilian, but that's far from the truth. You all definitely speak civilian," I said.

"Oh, we speak civilian, but the color of our blood flowing through our veins hasn't changed; it is and will always be red, white, and blue." Mason replied, with his voice changing while he was speaking. I could hear the overwhelming pride in his tone.

"Does Adam's blood have the same color?" I asked.

"Yes, he does. On this team, he better," Dante answered.

"Only he thinks he has ice water flowing through his veins, but from what we have witnessed lately, that is quite unlikely," Rocco added.

"I think of him more as a Slider," I said in response to the "ice water" comment.

"Nice *Top Gun* reference. I agree, Adam is definitely no pilot," Mason replied.

When Banks and Adam came back to the party, everything was cool. Adam walked passed us on his way to the bar and he didn't say a word.

"Kastle, can I have a word?" Banks said, as he pulled me aside.

"So, what's up?" I replied.

"I need you to do me a favor and do whatever you have to do to get along with Adam," Banks said.

"I have nothing against him and I will go out of my way to make peace. I just want to fit in and be a part of the team," I responded.

"I see the way you look at the guys; you look them in the eyes, while under Adam's regime, they are looked down upon. When it comes to leadership, not everyone has it; but, my friend you have it and then some. Kastle, I want you to lead these guys; give me a couple of months and then it's all yours," Banks said to me.

"I am cool either way; whatever you want. I am all yours," I replied, as we joined the others. All of us had a good time that night. I knew then, I was going to like working with them.

Chapter 5
The Tristan Lake Job

"Welcome to Miami Mr. Raines," the limousine driver was there to greet me, as I exited the plane. It was pretty cool. He was even holding up a piece of paper with my name on it. I flew down on Banks' private jet, about an hour before Tristan was scheduled to arrive. I went into the airport to meet Tristan; he was flying commercial. I stopped by the food court on the way to the terminal to get something to drink. When I reached his gate, he had just arrived. I went up to him and shook his right hand. "It is a pleasure to meet you! Here you go, I picked up a little something for you."

Tristan took a sip of the drink that I got for him at the food court. "A root beer float, how could you possibly know?" Tristan asked.

"You're good!" Tristan's famous girlfriend surprisingly replied, as she stood next him.

"I'm sorry. Kastle Raines, this is my girlfriend, Sophie Brees," Tristan said.

"It is a pleasure to meet you. I'm a big fan," I responded. Sophie was a gorgeous Soap Actress and is very popular, mostly because of her boyfriend.

"I have to go; my flight to Orlando is boarding. Take good care of him for me. I'll be back this weekend."

They said their goodbyes and we continued on our way to the limo, which was waiting for us outside the airport.

"She's finishing up her first movie role this week," Tristan said as soon as we left Sophie.

"Really, she's a good actress; I'm surprised that she hasn't been in anything before now," I replied.

"She has had opportunities in the past; but, she waited for something that she wanted to do," Tristan explained.

"So why a root beer float?" I asked.

"I haven't told anyone why I drink it after I fly; but, I'm curious how you know that?" Tristan said.

"I normally don't give up my source but, okay... you first," I replied.

"When I was young, I was extremely shy and I didn't talk too much around a group of people. I would stay away from any situation where I had to speak. Yet, my grandmother wouldn't let me take the easy way out. She knew I liked root beer floats, so she would make me recite something to her, looking in her eyes the whole time, before I could have one. One time she had her friends over to play card games and she had me stand in front and read the directions to them. I eventually grew out of being shy, and later overcame a brief period of stage fright. From then on, I always had a root beer float when I finish something that I don't like doing, like flying. I hate flying. Actually, flying is about the only thing that I dislike these days. Also, it's a superstition that reminds me where I started and how far I've come. All right, we had a deal. How did you know about this?" Tristan asked.

"My boss told me; it's unbelievable the information he can get. As for his sources, I don't know," I replied

"Banks Newman, I've only heard good things about him. That is why I was so shocked that he had someone like that working for him, when I used your company in the past," Tristan said.

"They're old friends. He sent me to repair the damage and begin a long lasting, business relationship," I responded.

"It's already one hundred percent better. I'm impressed so far," he replied.

We dropped off our luggage at the house before going to the set. Tristan rented a house right on the beach, not far from where he was working. The house was not that big, but it was really nice. I'm sure it was very expensive to rent. However, when you make twenty million per movie, it is affordable. He liked renting instead of hotels, if he was going to be in one place for months at a time. He owned a gigantic home in L.A. and an apartment in New York, his most common destinations. I stayed in the one bedroom, one bath guesthouse located by the pool and hot tub. After I went in and checked out my home for the next couple of months; I returned to the main house and then we were on our way.

We arrived on the set of his movie a few minutes after leaving his house. I was excited about being there; it was my first time on a movie set. I enjoyed my first day on the job immensely; the scenes were shot from a strip club. The name of the movie was *The First Lady*. It was about a young politician, who was running for President. Ultimately, he falls in love with a stripper/porn star. He is projected to win, however he chooses her over the presidency and withdraws from the race. It was somewhat of a chic flick compared to the action movies he usually does. He's a great actor, so it was not hard to pull off the transition.

When we were off the set, Tristan made it easy on me. He didn't go out every night; he was out of the clubbing stage. I caught him just at the right time; he was in a serious relationship. The only time he went out, was on the weekends that Sophie visited. He liked his privacy and the comforting factor that no one would know his business, at least from me. Banks had me sign a piece of paper that stated I wouldn't disclose any information to the press or anyone else.

On the first weekend that we were in Miami, Tristan had big plans. He chartered a yacht for the day and he hired a chef to cook dinner at his house for him and Sophie later that night. On Saturday, we arrived at the marina early to be ready before Sophie made it there. While we were waiting on board, the ridiculously exotic boat, we saw something interesting.

"Isn't that your boy right there?" Tristan said, as he pointed at two men going by in a speedboat.

"Yeah, that's Adam. Who's he with?" I said this with a surprised facial expression; I could see my reflection from the window that I was looking out of.

"Oh! I know who that is, someone I never cared to see again; his name is Ponce. He is a crazy fucker; he's one of the Cotto Brothers. I met him one night in a club about six months ago. He was there with Rushon Little," Tristan responded.

"The rapper?" I asked.

"Yeah, Rush used to sell dope for Ponce before he made it big. Ponce talked to me all night long; he was really intrigued with famous people and movies. He was drunk, so I don't know how much of it is true. He babbled about how the whole world would remember his name and he had plans that would make him famous. He told me how his father would put cigars out on him and his brothers' skin. He even showed me the burn marks. He described how their father tortured them and how they returned the favor before they killed him. Their father chopped off each of their little fingers, because he said they didn't need them."

"They have no pinky fingers?" I, surprisingly, asked Tristan.

"Rush told me that it's all probably true, the Cotto brothers are insane. He advised me and anyone else to keep their distance from every one of them."

"I'll find out why Adam's with him. Can you keep this between us?"

"You got it! Like I said before, I want nothing to do with either of them. But, in your case you should definitely watch out. Adam looked awfully cozy with someone who, without a doubt, should be avoided like a deadly plague," Tristan responded.

"I hear what you're saying. I'll check into it."

"Good! I warned you, that's all I can do. Now, let's enjoy this beautiful day."

"I agree. I'm going to get something to drink; do you want anything?" I asked.

"Yeah, I'll take a bottled water for now," Tristan replied.

"You got it!" I went to get two bottled waters. I returned a couple of minutes later, tossing Tristan's bottle towards him, and he instantly snagged it out of the air. We enjoyed a little sun before we went into the cabin to wait.

"So how long have you been doing this?" Tristan asked.

"Only a couple of months; but, I've been well trained."

"What did you do before?" Tristan asked.

"I played baseball," I replied.

"Really; who did you play for?"

"I was a pitcher for the Jacksonville Suns. In my last game, I threw a no hitter and I was headed to the Dodgers. That night, at a club, I met my girlfriend that I'm still with now. When I was leaving, I saw Sarah and her friend being harassed by some guys in the parking lot. I jumped in and took out three of them, but missed the fourth one that had the baseball bat. When I woke up, I was in the hospital and my arm was permanently fucked. It has healed; but my pitching days are over with," I replied.

"I am sorry, that really sucks. I go to games all of the time. I would love to have seen you play. I know it's not the same; but, if you're ever in L.A., I can get you on the field. You can throw batting practice or you can hit a few. My agent can hook it up for you. I got to do BP once and I had a blast," Tristan said.

"That's generous, but it still hurts a little. Later down the road, I might take you up on that though," I replied.

"Any time man, just give the word and you will be on the field in Dodger Stadium."

After a while, the boat captain and Sophie finally arrived and she wasn't alone; the woman standing next to her was so beautiful. They both had blonde hair, nice tans, and great bodies. They were about the same height; Sophie was slightly taller, but not by much. They looked like supermodels on a catwalk as they walked aboard, with their extravagant outdoor attire and expensive sunglasses. The captain assumed his position and we were off.

Tristan and I were in the cabin, waiting by the bar, as the girls made their way to us. Sophie ran into Tristan's arms and kissed him as if they had been apart for months.

"Kastle Raines, I want to introduce you to my best friend. This is Bianca Andrews," Sophie had a matchmaking grin on her face as she introduced us. I smiled as well; even though, I had a girlfriend. I was just being friendly. What can I say, beautiful women make me smile and these women were the definition of hot.

"Doesn't he have a smile that says he knows something everyone else doesn't?" Tristan pointed out to the girls. When Tristan said that, it reminded me of Bank's smile. Banks has that same look; I guess he had rubbed off on me.

"It is a pleasure to meet you Bianca," I said as we just shook hands; this being an extremely less dramatic greeting than Tristan and Sophie's.

"I hear that you are a psychic/bodyguard. Mr. Raines, what do I like to drink?" Bianca asked. She really put me on the spot; I had no clue what she liked. I had no time to research it, but I had to say something. I just tried to present it as smooth as possible.

"When you are at a bar you drink vodka and tonic, red and sometimes white wine with your meal, and champagne on occasion. When you are at home, you make margaritas or daiquiris. When you are outside in the sun you drink bottled water with your beer that is always in the bottle, never in the can." I then gave her a bottled water, followed by a beer; that I wrapped a napkin around, before handing it to her.

"Is all that true?" Sophie asked.

"That's amazing; you were real close," Bianca replied.

"Is my boy good or what?" Tristan said, as he gives me a fist bump.

"That was pretty good. Why don't you show me the rest of the boat, so we can give these two some time alone; and you can tell me how you knew all that?" Bianca said, as she opened the door and walked out.

"Okay, are you going to be okay in here boss?" I asked.

"Yes, he is. I'm all the protection he needs right now." Tristan gave me a nod to leave them alone while Sophie was speaking. I left out of the cabin to locate Bianca, but she was nowhere to be found. The yacht was huge; I finally found her on the top deck standing beside the hot tub. She was looking out over the water, deep in thought. I walked over and stood next to her.

"What are you thinking about?" I asked, as she began to speak temporarily gazing into my eyes and then looking out over the water. As she continued, I realized that she was rapping.

"I'm out on the water, out on my yacht. It's okay, copy me. Admire what I got!"

"What was that?" I asked. At that time I had nothing; she really caught me off guard when she began to rap. I didn't listen to much hip hop, but after hearing that I had to listen to that song. I knew it would be different than her version; she made it sound so sexy.

"'Admire what I got,' it is a new song that just came out this week," She replied.

"I haven't heard it yet. Who is that and what made you think of it?" I inquired.

"We heard it on the way here, but this amazing view reminds me of the video. The song is by Rushon Little and the name of his album is *Rush Lit*. I love it."

"I'll have to check it out; since it was the first rap song that I was ever serenaded to," I replied.

"I haven't started serenading you yet," she replied, as she smiled.

"I didn't picture you as a fan of hip hop," I said changing the subject quickly.

"What, you're not a fan of hip hop?" She asked.

"I like all music, depending on the mood that I'm in," I replied.

"I like everything; I just wasn't into love songs today. I broke up with my boyfriend not too long ago and I haven't done anything, but stay home, since then. Sophie, the good friend she is, invited me to come with her to have some fun and we listened to Rush all the way here. I didn't want to be a third wheel, but she told me Tristan had a cute bodyguard that I just had to meet. I'm sensing from the way you change the subject that you're not single," Bianca said.

"Very perceptive. Yes, I have a girlfriend back in Jacksonville. I have to say that I'm having a good time here with you today. I can't believe I'm getting paid to spend a day on a yacht and listening to rap music. What do you do for a living? Are you an actress as well?"

"I am a photographer for *Tress* Magazine. It's an up and coming women's magazine." Bianca answered.

"That's great. I have never read that magazine, but I'll have to check out your work sometime. Speaking of work, let me go check on Tristan. I'll bring you another drink when I come back," I said.

"Great! I will be out here," Bianca said, as I returned to the cabin. I found Tristan and Sophie sitting by the small bar. I walked over to the bar and began to fix Bianca's drink; and to get a bottled water for myself.

"Hey boss, should anyone be putting pills or anything in your drink?" I asked.

"No! Did you?" Tristan said as he turned and looked at Sophie with an angry face.

"No! I would never!" Sophie replied, as her eyes began to tear up.

"Well, it looks like you already did. We are fucking done! I don't ever want to see you again!" Tristan shouted, as he walked over to the sink and poured his drink out.

"Wait! He's lying!" Sophie screamed out, as she pointed at me.

"He is my bodyguard, he works for me! Kastle, will you escort Sophie to the Captain's quarters until we get back to shore? I don't trust her!" Tristan said.

I quickly intervened. "Whoa! Wait a second. I was only joking. Sophie didn't do anything; but, in the future, I will definitely let you know if anyone tries something like that."

"I knew you were kidding all along. Why do you think that I didn't call her a bitch? Believe me, that is the first word that comes to mind, if a pill was put into my drink. I can't believe I got both of you," Tristan replied, as he was laughing.

"I knew it. I was just going along with it," Sophie responded.

"Bullshit! I had you," Tristan said looking at Sophie.

"Okay, you had me. You're an asshole; I was almost in tears. I'm mad at the both of you; you both are assholes," Sophie responded, while Tristan made himself another drink.

"Well, you are a great actor, so I don't feel that bad. I just wanted to check in; I am going to leave you two alone now," I said, as I glance outside the cabin where I found Bianca sitting at a table.

"Go and talk to the beautiful woman out there. It looks like she likes you," Tristan said, as he took a sip of his drink.

"She's not the only one. I saw the way you were looking at her earlier," Sophie said, as she showed me her sexy matchmaking grin again. She couldn't stop smiling as I began to leave the room after that riveting performance by Tristan.

"I'll be out here, if I am needed," I said, as I closed the door and went to sit at the table with Bianca.

"Hello, handsome. What is this? I thought I ordered a beer."

"It's Sangria; my own personal recipe. Trust me... you'll like it," I replied.

"Mmmm, this is good. You know, I am really glad I came today. I'm having fun. I thought I was going to be a third wheel until only a few minutes before we got here," Bianca said, as she continued to sip on her drink.

"I'm having fun too. I'm glad you came; if it wasn't for you, I would've had a boring day," I responded, as I took a drink of water. There was a moment there, well, more like a minute or two, that there was an extended period of silence. I was looking out at the water, enjoying the view of that truly beautiful day.

"What are you thinking about?" Bianca asked.

"It is a nice day to be on a boat. Don't you think so?" I said.

"I hate it when you meet someone and the two of you are in completely different places in life. One has been burned and one is in love. However, you can't disregard what you see. The eyes don't lie; body language doesn't lie; all of the symptoms of something special are there, but no action can be taken. Don't you hate when that happens?" Bianca said, as she began to smile.

"Yeah I do, that has happened to me quite a few times. How about a toast? Here is to good timing and happiness in our future," I responded, as I raised my bottle of water and touched her glass.

"Cheers!" Bianca said, as she raised her glass and continued smiling.

"Cheers!" I replied, as we continued conversing and enjoying the day. We were out there all day and my bodyguard skills weren't needed the entire trip. There were some fans that shouted and waved at Tristan and Sophie, but they didn't try to come aboard. The paparazzi took a few pictures, but that was it. That day, I got a taste of the good life and I enjoyed every minute of it.

On Monday, I experienced the repercussions of being famous. On the front page of a tabloid was a picture of the four of us on the yacht. In big letters, it said Swinger's Party. In the article, it said Tristan Lake and Sophie Brees hosted an all day swinging sex party on a yacht in Miami. In the photo that was taken, Bianca was touching my forearm. It was completely innocent; I think at that moment she was just asking me to get her a beer while I was at the bar. It was unreal how quick the tabloids were, 48 hours hadn't even passed. After I saw this, I immediately called Sarah to prepare her for the tabloid. I really could not believe that this happened. I assured her that nothing happened and I was there only doing my job. She said that she understood and believed that nothing happened.

Later, Banks called to inform me that she was pissed. After, I had talked to her earlier that day; she went and bought a copy of the tabloid. She walked into Banks' office, with tears running down her face, and threw the magazine at him. She was upset with the picture and with the report that there was finger banging going on when one of the pictures of Bianca and I were taken. Also, she was mad with Banks for sending me to Miami in the first place. She felt a lot better when Banks told her he would fly her down for the weekend. I informed Tristan of the situation, and he insisted that I take the weekend off. He told me he had to meet the woman who made me pass up a chance to be with Bianca Andrews.

Sarah arrived on Friday and I had no idea what to expect. I am not going to lie; I felt some kind of connection with Bianca, but I did not act on it. I had strong feelings for Sarah and I can't imagine doing anything to jeopardize that in any way. Plus, it had been months since I had been alone with another woman, except for the mayor's wife; I think that had a little something to do with it. This was the first time we had been apart since we met each other. I had not been in many long, serious relationships, so all of this stuff was new to me. I did not know how we would feel when we saw each other and I was eager to see if anything had changed. I felt my true feelings would come, when I first saw Sarah; which would determine if our relationship could survive us being apart.

When she got there, it was like no time had passed; we were more in love than ever. We had a great time that weekend. Hanging out with movie stars was different than the usual and also pretty cool. Tristan and Sophie liked her and thought we made a great couple. However, Sophie did tell me when no one else was around that Bianca and I would have made a cuter couple. She was still looking out for her friend. That's what good friends do, so I did not have any problem with the comment. I just continued being polite and my charming self. Sarah visited a few more times, while I was working in Miami. We had become closer over the months we were apart.

The last day in Miami, finally, came. The movie was finished. Tristan and Sophie were going to Barbados on vacation; a post movie trip was a tradition of theirs. Tristan offered me a job to be his permanent personal bodyguard; it was a great and lucrative offer, but I had to respectfully decline. We wished each other the best, and agreed to keep in touch. Before I left for the airport, he gave me a gift that Bianca had sent; it was a Rush Little CD.

Chapter 6
The Wedding

I don't know what it is, about returning home from a trip. When you walk off the plane and see your loved one, it is like you are drawn together with an unexplained unbelievable force filled with emotion. You can almost hear music playing in the background. That is, what it was like, when I saw Sarah waiting for me. It felt great! Yes, I was in love.

"Hey baby!" Sarah said, as I approached her with open arms.

"Hey sweetie!" I replied, as she came into my arms and we engaged in an absolutely amazing homecoming kiss.

"I am so glad that you are back. Things can finally go back to normal," Sarah said, as we were walking along in the terminal.

"I am too. I've missed you," I replied. I took her hand in mine.

"I want you to prove it," Sarah said, as she tugged on the bottom of my shirt, maintaining her continuous sexy smile.

"That is exactly what I had in mind," I replied, as we both began to move a little faster toward the car.

After we left the airport, we were going to Rocco's wedding. He and his wife were renewing their vows; he had promised her the wedding of her dreams when they could afford it. Instead of going straight to the wedding, Sarah drove us home after our intense greeting back at the airport. Sex before the wedding was good news, since the odds were good that I would get some after the wedding. Homecoming sex is almost always a guarantee. Twice in one day; I, now, would have to rethink my stance on going away on a job. The day looked very promising in every way.

We arrived a little late, but it had not started yet. The ceremony and the reception were held at The White Room in St. Augustine, not that far south of Jacksonville. I was not in the wedding; because Rocco didn't have any groomsmen. He only had Mason as his best man. The ceremony was great. You could say, it was a dream wedding. I could see it on the face of each and every woman in attendance. It must have cost a bundle; Rocco definitely went all out. Of course, Sarah had that wedding-envy look in her eyes; but, she never said anything. The look was popular and noticeably seen among others around the room. At the reception,

Sarah and I had our first opportunity to greet the bride and groom.

"I wish you all the best," I said, as I gave the bride a two-cheek kiss and shook Rocco's hand. "Congratulations!" I said to Rocco, as he introduced me to his beautiful wife.

"Kastle Raines, let me introduce to you my beautiful bride Isabella."

"It is a pleasure to, finally, meet you," Isabella said with a permanent, radiant smile on her face.

"Congrats, Rocco. Isabella, you look so beautiful and your dress is gorgeous. I am really happy for you two," Sarah said, as she stood there overjoyed with their happiness.

"Let me steal the groom for a second. Hey bro, can I have a word," I said. I, then, pulled Rocco aside and handed him an envelope, filled with money. The night before, I researched Italian traditions and I found the custom of the buste. I saw it done in Mafia movies, but I did not know what it was called. I knew Rocco would appreciate it when I found it.

"The buste! Thank you Kastle, I didn't expect this from you. This feels a little heavy," Rocco said, as he looked in the envelope and then looked at me.

"That's how I roll!" I replied

"It looks like protecting movie stars is the way to go. But, this is nothing compared to what we will have soon. You have come back just in time; there is something big coming up," Rocco said, as his face lit up with excitement.

"Oh, Really!"

"Yes! We'll talk about it later."

"Isabella is gorgeous! Why in the hell do you mess around on her?" I asked.

"She made me promise that all of that will end today. I am now like you, a one woman man." We walk over to Isabella and Sarah. "Isabella, my beautiful bride, I will be back in a few minutes to start the festivities. We're going to find Banks; Sarah, please keep the love of my life company until I return. I love you sweetheart!" Rocco said, as we both give them a kiss and walk away.

"We'll be back soon baby," I said to Sarah as we walked away.

"It is time for your initiation."

"Initiation? What are you talking about?" I curiously asked.

"You'll see. I've been looking forward to this all day." Rocco said. Then, we made our way outside to the parking lot to find Banks, Dante, and Mason standing in a circle beside Banks' black Suburban. "Come on. It's time for the celebratory smoke," Rocco said, as we then joined the circle.

"How are my boys doing? I have missed you guys. I am so glad to be back!"

"Welcome back!" They all say to me. Banks comes over and puts his arm around me and talks to me.

"I told Rocco to bring you back here. We have a tradition that we take part in once a month. We get together before a job and pass around this joint; it is the only time it's allowed. We do it for luck," Banks said.

"I definitely need it today; I promised my wife no more straying," Rocco said.

"I love weed! We get baked once a month for luck and it's definitely something I look forward to," Mason explained.

"I don't do it; but, since it's tradition, pass it over here." Rocco finishes hitting it and passes the joint to me.

"There you go! Enjoy yourself Kastle, it's my wedding day. Congrats, you are now one of us," Rocco said, as I pass it along in the rotation. I never thought I would be passing Banks a joint.

"I thought this was a group thing. Aren't we missing one?" I asked everyone as Banks was hitting it.

"Yeah, our fearless leader!" Mason answered.

"Cut my man Adam some slack; he's a busy man," Rocco said.

"Rocco is taking up for Adam, what is this?" I asked in amazement. I was surprised by Dante's remark also; he usually defends Adam when he's not around. I guess the one joint had an effect on everyone in some way.

"What can I say; he sent me a nice sized envelope. Take this. I must have had too much." Rocco replied, as he dropped the joint momentarily; after the immediate recovery, he passed it along to Mason.

"Rocco, what is the Latin word for weed?" I asked, as I turned toward him.

"Hell if I know? Why?" Rocco responded.

"In weed there is truth. Instead of wine, weed makes Dante tell the truth. Didn't you hear him take a shot at Adam?" I said, referring back to Dante's fearless leader comment.

"Yes I did," Rocco concurred.

"Yeah, I caught that too. It must be that he's high; the only time he takes a shot at Marshall is to his face," Mason replied, as he hit the joint a few times and then gave it to Dante.

"It wasn't a shot at Adam: he is our leader and he is fearless. He's like Stone Cold with hair," Dante responded.

"Stone Cold? I don't see it; but, I'm not around him everyday like the rest of you," I replied.

"Well, I am and Stone Cold he is not," Mason added.

"I'm not even going to respond to that," Rocco said.

"Maybe that's a bad analogy. He's more like a caged animal that can't be tamed," Dante said, as he puffed on the joint and then passed it along to Banks.

"Wait, didn't the rotation get screwed up?" Rocco said.

"No, it is right!" Banks replied as he hit the weed.

"The caged animal has already been tamed by Kastle... twice," Mason said in response to Dante's new analogy.

"Let me stop now; this is wrecking my buzz," Dante replied.

"Your leader wanted to be here, but he had to finalize the details for our next job. The job is very important and it will make everyone here a lot of money. Adam meant no disrespect to Rocco or to the rest of you and he sent this fine herb to show that. He wanted everyone to enjoy themselves before next week. He is taking care of his soldiers." After Banks' statement, we could not hold back the laughter. Banks was not mad that we were laughing; he just had to take up for Adam in some way or the other. He knew we didn't always get along, but he would always have his guys' back; if they were present or not.

We returned to the party after finishing the joint; and what a party it was. Everyone had a blast; I highly recommend attending an Italian reception. Stoned or not, it was good times for everyone.

Chapter 7
Set for Life

This was the big day. I went to Banks' for breakfast. We had business to discuss before we met with the other guys. I did not know exactly what to expect and I had no idea what this job consisted of. Up to this point, I had been totally in the dark. When I arrived, there was a man there sitting and talking with Banks. They both eagerly stood up and greeted me, when I reached the table.

"Good morning!" I said, as I firmly shook both of their hands.

"It is a great morning, Kastle my boy. You are right on time. Can I get you a cup of coffee or espresso?" Banks said with a smile; I could even hear the excitement in his voice. Now, I was even more interested in what Banks and the other gentleman had to say.

"I'll just have orange juice," I replied.

"Banks your son-in-law is very punctual; but, he's not an espresso drinker," the man with him said, as Banks handed me a glass of orange juice before he returned to his seat.

"We were just talking about you. I want you to meet one of my closest friends, Arnold Franklin. To everyone that knows him he is known plainly as Gus."

"Kastle Raines. It is a pleasure to meet you, pal. Banks has bragged on you so much. Now I can put a face with the name that I hear so much about," Gus said.

"It is great to meet you, Gus," I said, as we exchanged pleasantries and he shook my hand once again. He looked a few years older than Banks, but he was still in fairly good shape.

"Gus handles all of our finances; he's the best. He will be taking excellent care of your money," Banks enthusiastically explained.

"I have your offshore account all set up; everything on my end will be taken care of. I will hide your money and you will never have anything to worry about. This is what I do and I get well compensated for my duties," Gus said, while occasionally sipping espresso from the cup he had in front of him.

"Gus is the best! Why don't you break it down for him? Are you sure you don't want any espresso? It will give you a jumpstart for the day," Banks said, as he got up from his seat to go and refill their cups.

"No, thanks. I'm okay," I said to Banks, as I then turned my attention back to Gus.

"Alright Kastle, this is how it works. All of your checks from Banks' security company, which you will receive from here on out, are deposited in your personal legit account. This money will be taxed, keeping the government happy and out of your business. I know you already have money from your baseball contract and I suggest you take some and invest in stocks or real estate. I can help you with all of it, just let me know. The offshore account is your crew account; any money taken out of this account has to be signed off by me. This is mainly for me to keep track of everything; we have to be on the safe side. Banks and I are like brothers, there is an understood trust between us; it is the same with all of the other guys. I hope this can be true with us, either now or in the future," Gus said, as Banks returned with two full cups of espresso that he set on the table.

"If Banks vouches for you, I can trust you too. This all sounds cool. I think my money will be in good hands. It is going be a pleasure working with you," I replied.

"Gus is a part of our crew; he's just not out in the field. He takes care of the money, yes; but he also helps with Intel and other aspects of the operations. Let's discuss the details of the job. Each one of you will be paid one million for one night of your services. This job is going to set me up for life. We do this, and then we are out. We go legit after this," Banks said this with a huge grin, as he and Gus continued to consume their coffee drinks.

Gus, always thinking of ways to make more money, informed me of my options. "Here's the deal. Unlike you, the others are tapped, they have no money saved. You can invest in this deal and make an extra four million, to give you five total. On each of the other three jobs, each of you will be putting up one million and getting five million in return."

"Sweet, I am in. Now, will you tell me how in the hell I will make eight figures in four nights?" I asked, as Banks began to enlighten me on the details of the job.

"My crew has overseen and guarded a number of shipments being brought into our country; making undeserving fuckers tons of money. Now, we will guard our own shipments. You know this shit will get here, if we do this or not. I just refuse to help these cocksuckers any longer. We will be bringing the shipments here to Jacksonville and supplying the entire southeast, excluding Florida. That is the deal we worked out. We can supply any other state with coke," Banks explained.

"So, we are smugglers?" I asked.

"Just for four nights. Trust me, we've covered everything, the plan is golden! We are all good! After we do this; we are on easy street," Banks replied.

"Okay, I think I'm ready for that shot of espresso now," I said.

"I knew he would convert!" Gus replied, as Banks placed the cup in front of me on the table.

"After I had to quit playing baseball, I never thought I would ever make another million dollars again. I am ready, let's do this. Are you coming with us, Gus?" I said, after I took the shot of espresso and returned the cup to its previous spot on the table.

"Gus will not be seen with you guys. You can see him here and only here. This is just in case something does happen," Banks replied.

"I thought you said everything is taken care of; that everything is all good," I said with sarcastic intentions.

"We are just taking every precaution; covering all angles, good or bad. We have everything under control," Banks responded, as he leaned back in his chair.

"Banks, it sounds like he's worried," Gus added.

"My future son-in-law is just being cautious; he's just like me. That's what a good leader should be. He should worry about his ass, along with his crew. This is a good reaction; it shows me that he is thinking about the future. He is thinking ahead and taking precautions to make sure that his wife's and children's futures will not be affected. This is good stuff."

"Yes it is, I'm sold on everything and I am anxious to get started," I said, after Banks' analysis was concluded.

"Well, let's go. Gus, I'll meet up with you later. Kastle, you ride with me." I finished my OJ, while they finished their espressos. Then, Banks and I were off to meet up with the other guys at the marina.

When we arrived, the guys were standing on the pier along side three fifty foot racing boats. "Hey boys! Are we ready to make some money?" Banks was really pumped. "Kastle and Dante, you two are in one boat; Rocco and Mason will be in another. Adam you will be going solo to Suge Island. You will get the boys loaded and bring the last load in your boat on your way back. I need your A-game tonight fellas! This is the big payday that we have been waiting for. Let's bring it home!" Banks forcefully replied.

"You heard the skipper; let's go. You girls just try and keep up." Adam always had to say something, so he would feel in charge.

"Dante, make sure Kastle is squared away. He'll need some gear; take care of him for me. Well, I'm out of here. Good luck men," Banks said, as he left us at the pier.

"How about we make a friendly wager; everybody will put up a grand, the winning boat gets 5 G's." We liked Dante's intriguing proposal; it made the trip more interesting. There is nothing wrong with betting amongst friends. It is fun; just an extra rush to add to our action packed days on our personal playground.

Before our friendly race began, Adam had to show us where the drop off point was located. It was ten miles up the coast, at a dock, behind an empty warehouse. Adam pointed out the destination as we were passing; we didn't want to draw any extra attention to ourselves by stopping. We were informed, later, that Banks was taking care of the drop off point; we just needed to know how to get there. Adam snapped a few pictures for us to examine later; then, the race was on. Dante and I started off with a lead that gradually increased more and more. Dante really knew what he was doing and I just let him do his thing. It didn't bother me to be a wingman; I can be a team player.

"You are killing them. The way Adam talked; I thought he was the one to beat." I said this to Dante with a strong wind hitting our faces.

"Banks has one like this; I borrow it almost every weekend," Dante said.

"This is going to be easy money for me; you've done all the work. Instead of splitting, you deserve a bigger piece. You take three thousand and I'll take two," I said.

"Okay, that sounds good to me; but, it's not over yet, Raines," Dante replied.

"Please! It's in the bag; I can see the Island from here. Why is it called Suge Island anyway?" We couldn't have been more than ten miles out at the time.

"In the 80's, it was the location of a cocaine party that took place every weekend, until it was eventually shutdown. It was like an 'underground rave' back then. In the newspaper, there would be an add for a five pound bag of sugar on sale for fifty cents every Thursday. On the weekend that there would be a party on Suge Island, the price would be fifty dollars. Which was smart; if anyone complained, it was just a misprint and no one thought anything of it. There was a party only once a month; so, there wasn't a misprint every week," Dante explained.

"That's brilliant!" I said.

"The name Suge came sometime after the weekend party was shutdown," Dante explained. This is when we were interrupted by Adam. Suddenly, he called off the race. He radioed to us, and said that he needed to be seen first by the suppliers. If they arrived early, he was afraid they might have itchy trigger fingers. We slowed down, and Adam led us to the island. When we arrived it was completely deserted. Adam stepped on the island like a proud explorer who had just made the biggest discovery in history.

"Well, it looks like no one is here. Can you guys find your way back? Make sure you guys are back here at 9:30," Adam said, as he began to walk off, leaving Rocco and Mason laughing at us. I looked at them with a slight grin and puzzled look on my face.

"What? You have got to be kidding me. Does he pull this shit all the time?" I said, as Adam stopped walking and turned around.

"You can't win all the time slugger," Adam responded, as he turned back around and continued to walk.

"You guys were shafted; but, you had to expect some type of payback after the beatings he's had," Mason said.

"You two are taking this better than I would have," Rocco added.

"What do you think about Stone Cold with hair, now?" I asked Dante.

"Yeah, it was a bitch move; even for him," Dante replied.

"Fucking right, it was a bitch move. Why would he do that? He gave me so much shit about 'a real man uses his right to shake hands' and 'a real man honors the bet that he made and doesn't pussy out at the last second,'" I replied.

"Around these parts, we follow the chain of command. Adam giving an order is like Banks giving it and he knows that. He abuses his power a little; but, that is just the way he is. It was only a grand. If it was more, trust me, we would have a problem," Dante said.

"It sounds like Kastle is trying to bring Dante over to our side," Rocco said, as he turned and looked at Mason.

"Yeah. He's on his way to converting," Mason added.

"I don't take sides; I always stay neutral," Dante responded.

"I don't care about sides. I got what I wanted; Dante calling Adam a bitch. I'm just glad that everybody can see, that he is a shady dude," I said, as we boarded our boats and headed back home. Upon arrival, we went our separate ways to get ready for the long night ahead of us. I grabbed a bite to eat and took a nap. While we were napping, Adam was waiting for the shipment to arrive. It would be there waiting for us; that is the way that Banks wanted it. Adam dealt with the suppliers and we were never to be seen.

We met back at the marina and set off on our mission. We arrived on Suge Island at 9:15 P.M.; which made us fifteen minutes early. Banks believed if you weren't fifteen minutes early, you were late. Adam and the shipment were waiting on us when we arrived. We loaded the three boats and waited for 10:00 P.M. There was a well planned schedule that we were following. At ten, our two boats headed to the drop off point and Adam stayed behind to watch over the shipment. He would bring his load at the end of the night. Adam guarded the cocaine with a small arsenal and we had something similar. When we reached the drop point; there were two vans there and no person in sight. We loaded the vans and returned to Suge. Once we were clear, we sent a text to a cell number that Banks had set up. This let the van drivers know to retrieve the vans and bring two more. Banks gave each of us two phones, so we would have at least one that worked. They were stolen, so nothing could be traced back to any of us. The plan was flawless and we executed it perfectly. The night was a big success, with no problems at all. Banks cashed in big time and I didn't do too bad myself. Five million for one easy night; that was awesome. The one million each of the others made was not bad either.

The next two nights went just as smooth as the first. Everything went according to plan; it was, without question, the easiest money that I had ever made. We were extremely pleased after we made another eight million on the two jobs; this was a sweet deal for everyone. The last job was coming up and then our smuggling days were over. The plan was the same as the previous three; except the time and the drop point, which always changed. There was a different drop point on each job; however, all were at an abandoned warehouse. The first load was to be dropped off at 3:30 A.M.

On the last job, everything went just as smooth as the rest. It was a small shipment, so all that was needed was a single trip. We arrived at the drop point, eagerly, wanting to get the job over with. We finished unloading two of the boats, when our leader had something to say.

"Listen up you guys; I want to say something. I really appreciate everything, each of you has done. I'm new at being in charge and giving orders. You knuckleheads could have made it hard on me; but, you didn't. I thank you for that. I know we don't always see eye to eye, but we worked together and this job is done. We are now fucking millionaires! To show my appreciation, I am going to unload my boat by myself. Let me get my hands dirty too, you guys are done. Go ahead and head back to the marina. Banks has rented out the bar for us. Here's the key, go ahead and get the party started; you guys deserve it. I'll be right behind you," Adam said. It finally looked as if he was coming around; well, at least he was improving his leadership skills.

We couldn't believe that Adam was doing this; but, we didn't give him a chance to change his mind. We hauled ass to the marina. It was four in the morning and this job was over; it was time to celebrate. Dante had the key; so, he approached the door first and opened it up for us. The place was all ours for twelve hours. We could have anything we wanted; we just had to help ourselves. Banks was picking up our tab for a job well done; it was definitely time to celebrate. I took the initiative and jumped behind the bar. I grabbed beers for the guys and started pouring shots. We were consuming a large amount of alcohol; you name it, we were drinking it. We were there for about twenty minutes, when there was a knock on the door. Mason answered the door and returned with four ladies. They were wearing short, skin tight dresses and they looked like strippers.

Mason presents the ladies with his arms around them and a big smile on his face. "Guys, Adam has provided us with entertainment. Ladies we will start the music, you can change in the rooms over there."

"Where is Marshall? He should have made it here by now." Dante was right; it should not have taken any time for Adam to unload his boat.

"Wherever he is, he's wet; it is pouring out there," Mason replied.

"You know Adam can be a real prick; but, I have to give it to him, he really came thru this time," Rocco replied.

"He's just trying to get you to cheat on Isabella, so he will have a shot with her." Mason always messed with Rocco about Adam trying to take his wife.

"That's the future mother of my children, asshole. Plus, I told you, I'm done with all that, and I meant it. You two can have all four of them. Kastle and I will enjoy the show, then go home to our beautiful, sexier women and let you guys worry about pissing razor blades in the morning. Before this thing gets kicked off, let's have a toast; break open the bubbly," Rocco said.

"There's no bubbly. How about a shot of Patron?" I responded.

"Patron in place of champagne, you've got to be kidding me." Nevertheless, Rocco raised his glass, as we all toasted to the completion of the very lucrative job.

"Alright Jacks, let's get this party started," Mason said to Dante.

"Yes, indeed. I am right behind you," Dante said, as the music began to play. Mason and Dante went over to the table to enjoy the show, while Rocco hung back with me at the bar.

"Why aren't you over there? You're not married yet, Kastle. No one here will rat. You can have all the fun you want. Well, Adam might; but, he's not even here yet."

"I can see everything from here. You know, it's funny that you mentioned marriage; it has crossed my mind quite a bit lately. I haven't started looking at rings or anything, yet; I'm just in the thinking stage."

"Believe it or not, I am all for it; marriage is great. If she's the one, then go for it. Think about it and make sure. Then, buy her a huge rock and don't look back," Rocco said, with a serious look on his face.

"I am surprised; that, my friend, was good positive advice. So, when is there going to be a little Rocco running around?"

"We've talked about it and we're thinking, probably, next year," Rocco replied.

"That's great, Rocco. Can I get you another drink?" I said.

"Sure, let me have a whiskey on the rocks. So! What's next for us? I know your future father-in-law has let you in on the future plans." I gave Rocco his cocktail, as I began to answer his question.

"He said that we are going legit. We are now law abiding citizens."

"Bullshit! He is just like the rest of us adrenaline junkies. We crave action and must have it in our lives, in some form or the other," Rocco responded.

"Don't you think we pissed off that somebody, who missed out on a ton of money? We never saw any one. There is no telling who the hell we were dealing with in each direction." It was something that had been on my mind, after the conclusion of the job.

"Banks was protecting us. The fewer people involved, the better," Rocco said, as he tried to put my mind at ease.

"Come on Rocco, you're not the least bit worried. Yeah, I trust Banks, but do you really trust Adam?" I asked.

"Yes he is a real cocksucker, but he doesn't have the balls to rat us out. Adam wouldn't do that to Banks," Rocco replied.

"I'm just saying, out of all of us, he is the only one I worry about. Come on, he knows all the parties involved. If someone wanted answers, who do you think they would get it from; him or Banks?" I said.

"You have a point, but I don't think we have anything to worry about. Now, we will have to get accustomed to being rich and having a boring job," Rocco said.

"I can deal with rich and boring," I responded.

"Here's to boring." We both raise our glasses and then proceeded to the table to enjoy a lap dance or two.

"It's about time my boys joined the party! I told Mason you two aren't whipped," Dante said, after we walked over and sat down.

"Oh, they're whipped! These girls are too hot, for it to take them this long, to get over here," Mason said, as two of the girls moved our way and commenced to entertain us. After the third or fourth satisfying dance, Rocco leaned over toward me and asked a question.

"You look preoccupied. What's wrong Kastle?"

"It is hard for me to relax until Adam shows his face," I said, while the girl was in the middle of another lap dance. "Don't get me wrong, I am definitely enjoying myself."

"Would you feel better if we called Banks? My cell is in Mason's Hummer. I'll go get it," Rocco replied.

"Yeah, let's see if Banks has heard from him; so, I can enjoy myself," I said, as Rocco left the bar and returned a few minutes later.

"There's a problem; you guys need to come with me," Rocco said, as my mind began to race; mostly with negative thoughts.

"Ladies, take a well deserved rest and we will be back soon." Mason was clearly enjoying himself. He was more concerned about the girls than our problem. We left the strippers in the bar, as we went outside and found Adam standing there soaking wet; even though it had stopped raining. He had his yoyo steadily going up and down, from the first moment I laid eyes on him.

"Adam, let me be the one to say thank you; the girls are awesome. I had my doubts, but you came thru big time. Now, why are we out here? There are strippers inside!" Mason said unexpectedly.

"Hold up Mason, you will want to here this." Rocco had a concerned look on his face when he spoke to Mason.

"This is going to be hard; I am so sorry!" Adam said.

"What are you talking about?" Dante took the words right out of my mouth. I felt my eyebrows raise.

"I should have kept you guys there until the job was complete. The load was jacked! At least five men wearing mask took the vans. They had the drivers tied up on the ground, and me at gunpoint. There was nothing I could do! One of them had a grenade and threatened to throw it in the boat if I didn't do what he said. I had to throw my guns and cell phone in the water. Plus, I had to rip the radio out and toss it, also. After they left in the vans, I found a payphone and called Banks. There is nothing he could do about the load. The pickup spot was set up there so the load could disappear as soon as possible. Banks is smoothing everything over with the buyers right now." We all stood there in complete shock at Adam's news.

"Are you fucking with us; this has to be a joke? Did Banks think of this or did you?" Rocco had the same thought as the rest of us; this couldn't be real.

"I wish it was a joke, but it's not. It is all my fault!" Adam replied.

"Damn right, it's your fault!" Rocco responded.

"Look, I never thought anything would happen. The plan was perfect! I am so disappointed, I just wanted to make Banks proud; he's like a father to me. And with you guys, I wanted to be a part of the team for once. I have always been the outsider with you. I was just trying to bring us closer together. Kastle is around for five minutes and it seems you guys have been close friends for years. Yeah, I am a little jealous; but, I do apologize for my actions. Kastle, I am sorry. For the longest time I wanted so much to be where you are; a part of Banks' family. I have accepted the reality of that never happening and I'm fine with it. I know I screwed up tonight and I hope you guys will forgive me. I will reimburse you for the money that was lost and even the money that was supposed to be made. I just want to make things right. Will somebody say something?" Adam said.

"I haven't known you for that long, but I never expected this. You sound sincere; so, I accept your apology and if you want forgiveness, you have it. It is unfortunate that this happened; but, it was a risk that we all took when we invested a million in this deal. However, I don't like to lose millions over a decision I didn't agree with in the first place. I do want the million I lost; the other four is unnecessary," I replied.

"You've got it!" Adam replied.

"This is business; so, I can't speak for everybody. You will have to ask them individually. As for you and I, we are all good. You guys talk it over and I will be behind the bar pouring us some shots. I am sure we all could use another drink. When all of the business is discussed, come join me when you're done." I went back inside and started pouring shots for the boys. I grabbed beers and had them setting on the bar when they arrived a few minutes later.

"Kastle, let me have a double shot of whiskey with this beer. Now, bring on the strippers!" Adam said, after he downed his shot of whiskey. He, then, took his beer and joined Mason and Dante at the table. Rocco stayed behind with me at the bar while we watched the show from there.

"So, did you guys work everything out?" I asked Rocco, while we were sitting at the bar.

"Yes, we did. After your speech, Mason and Dante asked for a million. I made him cough up five," Rocco said.

"So, you made him pony up the full amount," I replied.

"Yes, I did; I didn't agree with the decision either. The prick has busted my balls non stop for years. I have no sympathy for him. Like you said, this is business; he should not have offered," Rocco responded, and then turned up his beer.

"Hey, I completely understand where you are coming from; I'm usually the same way. I guess I am feeling generous today. Any other time, I would have made him shell out the full amount. How about a toast? Here is to now having more money than Adam," I said, as we raised our beers.

"I will drink to that. Salut!" Rocco replied.

Chapter 8
Strike Day

It began like a regular day. Sarah and I woke up early to go to work. Sarah was very excited because it was the first day of school and she really loved her job. Plus, it had been a long summer and she was starting to get a little bored. As for me, I actually had something constructive to do that day. Usually, I would workout, play golf, or go to the shooting range; basically, just hang out with the guys all day. We had been on easy street since our big payday. Everything was great; life was real good. Things changed after the night at the marina; Adam was starting to fit in with the rest of us. Banks looked like a proud poppa when he saw how well we were getting along; that is, after the initial shock began to wear off. On this day, Mason and I were recruiting a guy to work for RB Security. He lived about an hour south of Jacksonville. Mason arrived just as Sarah was about to leave for work. I walked her to her car, wished her good luck, and kissed her goodbye. While walking toward Mason's Hummer, I waved at Sarah as she drove off.

"I'm impressed. I didn't expect you this early," I said, as I opened the door to find Mason wearing a pair of sunglasses that was similar to the ones I had on.

"Just get in superstar; you can praise my punctuality on the way. I am always on time, it doesn't matter how much I partied the night before; but, you wouldn't know anything about that married man."

"Please! I just found what I have been looking for. If it wasn't for Sarah, I would be right there with you." I responded. We were now on our way and decided to make a pit stop to get coffee at Coffee Ville before leaving Jacksonville. I noticed a flower shop next door as we pulled up. "I'll spring for coffee, if you go in to get them. I need to go in there and send Sarah some flowers on her first day of school." I handed Mason a twenty, when he agreed with my plan.

"What kind of coffee do you want?" He asked, as we opened the doors and started to get out of the vehicle.

"Just get me whatever you are having," I said.

"You got it," Mason replied, as I went in the flower shop and placed my order for a dozen roses. The delivery guy assured me the flowers would arrive at the school as early as possible. After doing my good boyfriend deed for the day, I met up with

Mason at his car. He handed me a coffee as soon as we got into the Hummer.

"What kind of coffee is this? And where is my change?" I asked.

"It's a latte and the change is for the flying fee," Mason said, as he turned the key and started the engine.

"What the hell is a flying fee?" I curiously asked.

"The flying fee is the payment for someone fetching something for you; in your case, a latte." Mason explained, as he now had us on our way to our destination.

"Your latte is your flying fee. Okay, just keep it! Drinks are on you later, just as soon as we're done."

"Cool, I know a place. There's a sweet spot right outside the university that has an abundance of college honeys at all hours of the day," Mason said, with a big smile.

"Beautiful scenery, on a Monday, there is nothing wrong with that. Anywhere you want bro; just have me back by five o'clock," I responded, as I sipped on the latte.

"Scenery, look just play along and I will bring Jacks back with me. I know he's down," Mason replied.

"Dude, it is 8:30 in the morning and we just made it out of Jacksonville; let's get through the day first and see how it goes. But, I do like your positivity," I said. We both listened closely to the radio when they began an announcement that stated many officers of the Jacksonville Police Department were on strike as of 8:00 A.M.

"Why are they striking? I have never heard of a police strike," I said to Mason.

"There were two incidents, last week, involving a group of teenagers almost beating a cop to death. The two cops were suspended for hitting the, so called, innocent bystanders and on both occasions the teenagers were not charged. They walked out because of the suspension of the cop that was defending himself," Mason replied.

"Good for them. You have to look out for your family," I said, as we continued to talk. This helped to pass the time on our road trip. "So why did you ever get out of the military?" I asked.

"I did my time and it was great for me; but, I knew from the first day, I wouldn't make a career of it."

"If you knew from the beginning, weren't there ways to get out?"

"Sure, there was ways to get kicked out. However, I could handle four years; just not decades. Once, I was coming back from overseas and we caught a ride back to the states on an aircraft carrier that was returning from a six month deployment. I was only onboard for three days, but I saw this black kid everywhere I went. They said he had only been on the ship for about a month and he was already getting a medical discharge. Everywhere this guy went, he was bouncing an invisible basketball. If he moved he was bouncing the ball, when he was sitting at the table eating, he would still bounce his ball. When he slept, his arm would be cradled like he was holding a basketball. The doctors finally came to the conclusion that he was nuts and he was granted a medical discharge upon arrival back in port," Mason said.

"That's crazy," I replied.

"Once we arrived, I was standing in line to get off the ship. In the Navy, you have to salute the officer and ask permission to go ashore. This kid was about five places ahead of me in line. He was still bouncing his ball as he saluted the officer and walked off about ten feet, and stopped. He did a crossover dribble with his invisible ball and then he shot a fade away jumper in to an invisible goal in the sky. Then he skipped off with his discharge papers under his arm," Mason said, as we both began to laugh.

"Now that's funny! Classic!" I replied. This was about the moment that we heard the news announcement on the radio. Normally we would be bumping a CD on Mason's system instead of the radio; because of Mason's story it just so happened that we were listening to a local radio station. In the middle of a song the shocking news was announced. "We have just received word that there has been an explosion at a school; it has not been confirmed, but one report has stated it was a bomb." At that moment, I began to get a little worried. Mason immediately looked at me when we heard it.

"I'm turning around. Let's, at least, check it out," Mason said, as we both stayed calm without jumping to any conclusions.

"I'll call Banks to see if he's heard anything." I got Banks' voicemail, and there was no answer at his house. "There's no answer." While I was on the phone, Mason was scanning the local stations for more information; and driving as fast as his Hummer could go. It seemed like after each second would pass, we both were getting more and more worried. Then, there it was on 93.3 FM. I only remember that because I was staring at the radio for what felt like an eternity. "It has been confirmed that a bomb has gone off at the West Healey Elementary School. Medical, fire and rescue teams are on scene. We will pass along more information just as soon as it comes available." I completely went numb. Several seconds of silence went by with Mason deciding what to say, while I was in a state of shock. All I could think about was Sarah and how the bombing had something to do with the hijacked shipment.

"Take me to her," I demanded.

"Let's be positive man, she could still be alive. The explosion could have been a car outside or something; you know how the media likes to jump the gun without getting all of the facts," Mason said.

"I pray she is okay, but I just have this bad feeling that she's not. I can't believe that this has happened! Mason, promise me that you will help find whoever did this and we will make them pay," I said.

"We are dealing with monsters, blowing up a school; breathing air is too good for them. I just hope we find them first." Mason's cell phone rings, Rocco calls to pass along more details and orders from Banks. "There was an explosion, it was a bomb, and it is bad. We are all meeting at Banks' house until we find out more information and we get further instructions," Mason said, as we took a detour around the school. There was really nothing we could do there anyway. Mason gets us to Banks' front door just a couple of minutes after talking to Rocco. Dante and Rocco were waiting in the living room glued to the TV. Every news station was covering the bombing, including the national news. When we walked in, I saw the video footage of the school. All you could see was a building in shambles. There was no footage of the bomb going off, but the video of the aftermath was heartbreaking enough. We all just sat around and watched, not saying anything. The only reports of the Police Strike that was in full swing were in small letters at the bottom of the screen. There were extra F.B.I. Agents and Sheriff's Department personnel taking up the slack for the strikers. Banks arrived; the door opened rapidly and he walked into the room at a fast pace. He had a worried look on his face, but we all did.

"Let's pray she is found and she's okay. The best way for us to help is find the people who did this. We have some information that Gus and Adam are checking on. If it's real, they will call you; so, be ready. It is time to man the fuck up; we can't let them get away with this. Strike or no strike, let's get to them first; let's find them and we're gonna kill'em. I'm going to the school to see about my little girl. I trust you four will take care of this," Banks said, as he pulled me to the side and puts his arm around me. "I know you want to go with me, but we really need to find these people. Hang in there and just think positive. If there is any news I will let you know as soon as I can," Banks said, as he walked out of the door.

Banks headed to the school, while we waited for Adam to call and continued watching the news coverage on the TV. It was truly heartbreaking and astonishing. There are really no words to express what we were seeing and feeling. At that time all we were able to see were mainly shots of the school in shambles, and a few tear-jerking images of the bodies of children being pulled from the smoky, soot-filled rubble. I remember sitting there focused on the fifty inch plasma, when we got the call. Adam informed us of the location of the suspect; according to the Intel he and Gus received, it was just one person responsible for the days' events. We exit the room giving a last glance at the TV, leaving the images imprinted in our minds as we departed. I walked with the guys out to Mason's Hummer, when I got a shocking surprise as we stopped at the back of Dante's Tahoe. Banks had Dante and Rocco make a pit stop to pick up a few things before coming to the house. In the back of the SUV contained one of everything; there was everything from grenades to rocket launchers back there. We quickly transferred the small arsenal to the Hummer and went on our own personal manhunt.

I rode in the back with Dante, Mason was the usual wheelman, and Rocco had shotgun. Adam said that our guy was on his way to St. Augustine; there was a private jet waiting for him. We were to get there as soon as possible and wait for an exact location. St. Augustine was about forty miles away, so we had a little time before we made it there. I had a few questions I was curious about. Up to this point their military history had been vague.

"So, what exactly did all of you do in the military?" I asked.

"Yes, we have. Aren't you asking if we have killed anybody?" Rocco said, as he turned around in his seat and began to give me some answers. "We were all special forces, but different units. Banks had worked with each of us at one point and brought us all together. It was a part of the job; we were given a mission and we completed it, by any means necessary."

"Why did you get out of it?" I just kept it short; I didn't want to pry too much.

"We wanted to spend time in the country we have served for years. We like it here; plus, getting shot at gets old. It was time to enjoy this great country of ours." Dante gave me a politically correct answer and I didn't expect anything less coming from him. I really wanted a particular reason, but I took it that it was time to change the subject. About this time, Gus sent us all a picture, of the guy we were looking for, to our phones.

"Ponce Cotto! The Cotto brothers control most of the drugs smuggled into Florida. It does make sense that he is responsible." Dante was just letting me know who he was; he didn't know that I already knew him.

"I saw him with Adam when I was in Miami. Do you remember when I was with Tristan

Lake, and the Paparazzi took pictures of us on a boat? It was that day."

"Oh yeah, I remember the hot blonde incident. We guarded a few shipments of his around that time. It makes sense, but it's hard for me to believe he could be this cold blooded. He's a major whack job, but it seemed like he would try to blow us up, before he put a bomb in a school. Stop! Stop the car! Pull over, but don't kill the engine. Pop the hood!" Rocco yelled, as Mason quickly pulled over and Rocco jumped out. He began to franticly search underneath the vehicle and under the hood. He couldn't find anything; I think he just talked himself into the idea of a bomb in the truck. He gets back in and closes the door. "I was being careful, you just never know about a person; especially Ponce."

"Are you okay?" Mason said, as he looked over with a surprised look on his face.

"Yes."

"Are you sure?" Mason asked.

"Yes! Drive! Fuck you guys! I just got this feeling and I trust my instincts; that's how I have lived for this long, but I'm glad I was wrong. You should be glad that I was worried about you ungrateful assholes."

"Good looking out, Rocco." Dante thanked him and patted him on his shoulder.

"We appreciate it." I showed my gratitude and put out my fist that he quickly bumped. Feeling left out, Mason wanted a fist bump too.

"Good looking, bro!" Mason said, as Rocco finally granted him a fist bump.

We made it to St. Augustine a couple of minutes later. I called Adam to get confirmation that our guy would be at the airport; it's a good thing I did. He informed me that he was at a strip bar on East 23rd Street. The game plan was for me to go in and make sure he was in there; since I was the only one he had never seen before. I wasn't totally sure that he didn't know who I was, so I tried to keep my distance and not let him see me. I walked in and paid the ten dollar cover charge to the girl in the front. I gave her an extra twenty to walk in before me to shield me from all the dudes looking when the door to the room opened. She was thrilled to make twenty dollars just for walking to the bar and back to the front door without having to shed any clothing. We walked in and she said something to the bartender. I spotted Ponce and we walked out. I accomplished my goal and returned to the parking lot to workout a game plan with the boys.

"He's in there. What's the plan?" I asked the guys, who were certainly more experienced in this sort of thing.

"We watch all of the exits and wait. We capture the target before he reaches his car and make sure we are not seen." Mason clued me in on our objective.

"Make sure he doesn't get to his car; a Lamborghini being chased by Mason, he will be in the air before we make it to the airport." Rocco had to, as he would put it, bust his balls a little bit.

"That's what those grenades are for," Mason replied, as he turned and looked at Rocco.

"If he gets in the air, I've got something for him. I have been dying to use the rocket launcher back there. Let's don't let it come to that, I want to have a chat with him first."

"We all want to log in a little face time with the fucker," I replied.

"Gus traced that Lamborghini over there back to him. He rented it in Jacksonville two days ago with a credit card that had a fake name on it and he used the ATM inside here with a debit card under the same name." Dante was updating me on Gus's Intel.

We continued to wait in the parking lot of the strip bar. Dante reached in the back of the Hummer and got a device along with a black bag. The device was a cell phone jammer that he gave to Mason to turn on. He handed Rocco a roll of duck tape and each of us a couple of plasticuffs, along with black gloves that were in the bag. He then got out and went to the back of the H2. He handed me two M4 assault rifles and four bulletproof vests over the seat. He closed the door and returned with a slightly bigger black bag. Dante opened the bag and gave us all a 9mm with extra clips. We kept the two M4's in the back with us. I could feel the adrenaline starting to pump as I was putting on the vest. This was starting to feel real; something was about to happen.

There were two empty spots open on the left side of the Lamborghini. Mason backed into the parking spot one over from his car, so we would be facing the building; therefore, setting up our escape route. The windows in the H2 were tinted, except for the two front ones. Mason set his seat way back; so, at first glance you could not see anyone waiting in the vehicle. Rocco joined us in the back seat, which was protected by the dark tint. He wasn't too happy about sitting bitch; but, him being a tad smaller than the three of us, it made for the best execution of the plan and the most sense.

About fifteen minutes had passed, when the front door opened and Ponce Cotto walked out. He continued toward us. Once he was a couple steps away from his car, I stepped out of the H2 setting the plan in motion. I walked around the back and quickly rushed Ponce with my gun drawn; we met at the door of the Lamborghini. I point the 9mm at the middle of his chest; shockingly, the cocky prick did not resist and presented me with an ultimatum.

"You must not know who I am! Drop your gun or you are dead! I'm feeling generous; you can follow me to the airport. I will leave the keys in the car and you can have it. You should do this; you can save your life, your family's life, and everyone you know." I did not say anything to him; I just stared and pointed my gun at him. Mason pulled around and stopped at the Lamborghini. Dante and Rocco jumped out of the back seat. Ponce turned around to see what was going on.

"I know you!" Ponce said, identifying Dante and Rocco immediately. At this time, I figured if he had any kind of a weapon he would have shown it then. Preoccupied with the identification of the other guys, I took this opportunity to take him down; I really put him on his ass. He had taken a half of a step towards the

Hummer, when I, cautiously, slid my right arm underneath his arm and put my hand on his chest. Then, using all of my strength, I slammed him to the ground with a little help from a leg sweep. He was definitely dazed when his head hit the asphalt. It was easy for us to get the plasticuffs around his wrists and ankles; he hardly put up a fight. Rocco put a rag, drenched with chloroform, over his nose and mouth to assure we would have a nice quiet ride to our destination. Dante tosses a black body bag on the ground that Rocco straightened out; and then gets the keys out of his pocket, along with his cell phone. After that we all picked up his lifeless body and stuffed it in a body bag, then put it in the back of the H2.

"Toss his ass in there. Let's roll!" Mason said, as we were putting Ponce in the Hummer. I rode with Dante in the Lamborghini, while Mason and Rocco followed us. Dante handed me the cell phone he got off of Ponce, so I could get his number from it. I found the cell number and sent it to Gus using my phone. Gus could find out who he had been talking to a lot easier than I could by calling each number that was listed. Plus, we didn't have much time; just in case, someone was using GPS to track it. We dumped the car in a deserted alley because we did not want anyone looking for the car to ask questions at the strip club. Someone could have noticed me in there and linked me back to Ponce's disappearance; we just tried to cover every angle. There was no need to wipe down the car since we were wearing gloves. There was nothing else for us to do but get in the back seat of the

Hummer. Mason gassed on it and had us on our way. Once we got pretty close to the airport we tossed the phone before we headed north.

By this time, all law enforcement and various government agencies were in a statewide search for the piece of shit that we had in our possession. There were road blocks along with the manhunt to be concerned about.

"What are we going to do if we hit a road block? Just hand him over? " I asked the guys, after hearing about the search on the radio.

"Negative! That's not an option. Banks will have a face to face with him first," Rocco said, in response to my question.

"Hell, I want a face to face with him," was my reply.

"We all want to be in his face. We need Gus; let me give him a call, so he can navigate us to our destination." Mason agreed with us, and he had a solution to our problem.

"Let your co-pilot do it; I will call Gus. You concentrate on the road." Rocco always wanted to feel useful and for the most part he always was. He called to see where we were going and to get the route we were going to use. Gus had a course plotted for us to reach an empty warehouse, that was close to the water and that had already been searched. He stayed on the line to walk Mason thru any obstacle he encountered with the assistance of his co-pilot, of course. We arrived at the warehouse at 2:00 P.M.; just in time before the chloroform was supposed to wear off. Dante and I opened the revolving doors to the warehouse, so Mason could drive in. We unloaded the body bag and contemplated our next move. Mason and Dante took his body out of the bag and placed him on the floor. The first thing I noticed was the Omega Deville watch he was wearing, along with his designer clothes; the piece of shit had good taste.

"I'm going to call Banks to see if he knows anything about Sarah and what we're doing with him." I walked outside, to the back of the building, to make the call. I dialed Banks' number and waited for him to answer.

"Kastle!" Banks answered the phone in his regular deep voice. I couldn't tell if he was happy or sad.

"Please tell me you have good news," I said, as I was hoping for the best.

"Kastle, I hold in my hand a ring that I pulled off my wife's finger when she was taken from me." I began to hear a crack in his voice; a tear began to run slowly down my face. "I just had to take it off my daughter's finger when I identified her body. Sarah is gone. I am in so much pain right now, as I know you are." I couldn't say anything; I was completely stunned. "We have to stay strong for now. There will be time to mourn after we make this right," Banks said.

"No! I can't believe this!" I replied.

"I know. It's hard to grasp that all of this is real," Banks responded.

"What is our next move? Are we going to turn him over to the authorities?" I asked, as I concentrated on the task at hand.

"Fuck No!" Banks replied.

"I'm glad to hear it; because, we didn't want to have to disobey a direct order," I responded.

"You boys get all the information you can out of him and then you execute him; that cocksucker killed my little girl. Make sure it can't be traced back to us. Be smart," Banks said, as he gave me direct orders.

"Banks, there is so much I want to say to you; but, right now, I am lost for words. I'll come see you when it is done."

"Okay, but please take your fucking time. I'm thinking of a long torture session with the prick hurting every second until his pathetic life comes to an end. Make that motherfucker feel some of the pain we are feeling. I'll see you when you get here." I got off the phone with Banks, still in disbelief. I leaned against the wall and stood for several minutes, trying to regain my composure before I returned inside. Once the sadness that I felt had turned into anger, it was time to go back in.

I went back in, full of rage and anger; as I walked toward them, I saw something that made me smile, but it only lasted for a second. I saw a rope draped over a beam with the two ends of the rope tied to the wrists of Ponce; his arms were stretched directly above his head. All of his weight was on his left leg; his right foot was placed behind his left knee and firmly tied. He was making sounds through the duck tape while attempting to escape from the situation, but the restraints were secure. He wasn't going anywhere. I could tell, even with the duck tape over his mouth, that he was pissed. His wardrobe, that cost well over a thousand dollars, now had green spots all over it; he was covered from head to toe.

"What is this?" I said, as I walked over to Mason and asked him what Rocco and Dante were doing to the guy.

"We had to wake him up; this is our way of doing it. It's your turn next; I know you want a piece of him," Rocco said, as we stood there watching them shoot at Ponce using paintball guns. They were really giving it to him nonstop.

"Kastle, come get you some!" Dante spotted me and wanted me to have a shot at him. I went over and joined Rocco. I have to admit it felt good shooting his dumb ass, even though we were just using paintballs. I shot him a number of times, ranging from his forehead to his left shin. When we were done, his entire body was well covered from head to toe.

"I need to talk to you guys." Rocco and I walked to where Mason and Dante were standing. "Banks saw Sarah's body, or what was left of it; she is fucking gone."

"Kastle, we are so sorry. She was like a sister to me; to all of us. Please tell me that Banks gave the order to whack this cocksucker." They all were thinking alike. Rocco just spoke up first, like he usually does.

"I'm sorry Kastle," Dante added.

"We all are sorry; if there's anything we can do," Mason said.

"We are to get all the information we can, before we end it; leaving no DNA evidence or anything else that can be led back to us," I responded.

"That is what we thought; we've already put our torture techniques into motion," Dante responded, along with an evil looking grin on his face. We walked over to Ponce to interrogate him; eager to get this over with. He had been eyeballing us for a while; it looked like he had something to say. Rocco ripped the tape off his mouth in a quick and forceful motion, to get it started. Ponce chuckled when the tape was removed.

"I love Americans, you are nice. There was even a nice American who helped me carry the bomb into the school. I was worried about asking him, but you Americans are always helping everybody, even me. You American cunts are wasting your time; you can't make me talk! I'm not a weak American, I will not break! Kill me! All of you will be dead soon..." Rocco reapplied the tape to his mouth to shut him up; and then loudly replied to Ponce's rant.

"We will see who is weak, you foreign cocksucker. You will regret ever setting foot in this country."

"Fuck you and your brothers; and whoever else that were involved with the bombing. We are about to go old school on your terrorist ass." Mason gave him his message, just before he rocked him with a right hook; that instantly, left a mark on his left cheek. It really sounded off when it landed; you could hear a bone break.

After Ponce's comments we all wanted a piece of him. We each took turns whaling on him; we really worked him over pretty good. He took numerous shots to the face, the gut, and the kidneys. His face was bloody and was beginning to swell; and we had only just begun. We all had heard the stories of how the Cotto brothers were tortured as kids; so, a part of us thought Ponce was right, but we had to try. He took American lives that day; he took Sarah from me. Oh, he would feel some pain before we were done with him. Mason grabbed a stick and began to hit his knee; mostly in the back of it.

"The key is to make him as uncomfortable as possible. Hitting the back of the knee, then tapping the knee cap and the sides of the knee will cause inflammation under the knee cap. There will be nonstop discomfort as long as he stands." Who knew, if what Mason was saying was true; but hey, it sounded believable. We continued pounding on him until Rocco became freaked out from Ponce starring at him.

"He's freaking me out with the staring, get the duck tape."

"I've got something for him. I'll be back," Mason said, as he tosses the roll to Rocco before leaving us. Rocco tears off a nice size piece and places the tape over his eyes.

"That's better." The staring didn't bother me, but the tape made Rocco feel at ease. I just wanted the duck tape to rip off as many eye lashes and eyebrow hairs as possible. I just thought that it would lead to some sort of discomfort. I know that is weak. The whole torture concept was new to me; I did not know where to start. What can I say; I was learning on the fly. I had numerous hardcore ideas that I would have loved to use on that guy, but I was unsure of the most effective methods to apply that would produce the information we wanted. When Mason returned I gladly ripped the tape from his eyes; as I examined the tape there were quite a few hairs stuck to it.

"What do you have there?" I curiously asked Mason, as he tossed the substance in Ponce's face and into his eyes.

"Acid!" Mason said, with a smirk on his face, as Ponce was screaming in pain.

"Acid doesn't scare me. I've been forced to drink it for years," Ponce said.

"Jesus! Mason, you are ruthless. Dude tell us something, I don't want to watch this!" I was really uncomfortable seeing acid being thrown in someone's eyes; but then, that's why it is called torture. It is hard for anybody to watch something like that; it would take a sick individual to enjoy torturing a person.

"It's shampoo; like there would be acid just lying around outside," Mason said, as he tossed the bottle aside.

"So there was a bottle of shampoo just lying around; that's really hardcore," Dante said to Mason.

"It was in a trash can next door; it was all I could find," Mason replied.

"He's not going to tell us anything and hitting him with paintballs, along with putting shampoo in his eyes, will not make him take us serious. Come on, he has killed Sarah and innocent children. I want to see all of his fingers and toes spread all over this warehouse. We should take him apart piece by piece!" I said, trying to speed up the whole process.

"I agree, but we do have some human compassion; it is hard to torture another human being under any circumstances," Dante said in response to my statement.

"We are just getting to the good part. Alright Kastle you're up; let's see what you've got," Mason told me.

"Drop his pants and shoot off his nuts, one by one; or we could use a knife. How would you like that, you cocksucker?" Rocco yelled at Ponce and voiced his suggestion. I walked closer to where Ponce was standing, restrained and still on one leg.

"I like it. That's a good idea," I replied as I stood in front of Ponce starring at him. After contemplating my next move, I then pulled my gun and stuck it in the middle of his right hand that was tied over his head; then pulled the trigger, sending an abundance of satisfaction through me. I rip the duck tape off his mouth to see if he has anything to say. Before he spoke he screamed out in total agony.

"Your mothers are whores!" I quickly went behind him and put my gun up to his foot and fired. He immediately lets out a loud painful cry. I then returned, to the spot directly in front of him. to listen to what he had to say.

"Fuck your mothers!" Ponce responded angrily.

"Wrong choice of words Cotto; talking about our mothers earns your ass another bullet." Mason, being true to his word, takes his 9mm and shoots Ponce in his left hand. He again cries out in pain; it continues for a little bit longer this time. His left leg was starting to noticeably shake; the discomfort he felt was turning to pain. Mason's methods were beginning to work; I have to admit I had my doubts at first. Then something surprising happened, Ponce began to speak.

"I see now you will not stop until you get what you want. I want this to be over; you can kill me or let me go. This was my purpose on earth; to carry out this order. The bomb was the beginning of many steps to our future that will result in the growth of my countrymen. I was trained for this act all my life. I don't see the order, I hear it and I do it, I win and I am rich. I love America. I would have loved to have been a citizen; I would have fought for this country like you will have to." At this point, he started talking crazier than he already had. I guess he was starting to lose blood or he was on crack or something. "I loved the power of my actions; but that's all I know. I respect you beneath me; you are men. I warn you helpers; he will come and bring the worst day the U.S. has ever seen with him. Let me down from here, and sit me in a chair! This only the beginning, I will tell you everything." We all agreed to let him sit in a chair; maybe he was telling the truth and we could get information from him.

"I will cut him down." Rocco takes his knife and starts to cut the rope when a gunshot goes off and a bullet hole appears in the middle of Ponce's forehead.

"You motherfucker!" Rocco, outraged that a bullet came inches away from him, quickly ran in our direction. We turned around and saw Adam lowering his gun. Dante catches Rocco before he reached Adam and holds him back before he could hit him.

"Let me go! He could have shot me; you know his aim sucks," Rocco yelled.

"It was an order from Banks and I am a sharpshooter; I don't miss you Italian prick. If you want to go, here I am. I'm not going anywhere?" Adam tossed his gun to the floor as he talked to Rocco. As soon as he dropped the gun, I dropped him. I stuck him with an overhand right, just below his left eye.

"Why do you guys always have to grab me, Kastle? For once, I wanted to be the one who hit him," Rocco said.

"I'm sorry, Rocco; my hands were free. Adam you could have waited one minute; he was finally talking," I said.

"You could have waited five fucking seconds to let me get out of the way, you dumb cocksucker!" Rocco replied.

"I received my orders and we were short on time," Adam said.

"I call foul! You should have spoken before we heard the gunshot," I replied.

"You should have walked a little closer," Dante added.

"Fuck you! I have had enough; this is it. I can't stand this piece of shit," Rocco said, as he continued to try to get close to Adam; but Mason and I held him back. Dante had hold of Adam. He was really upset so we had to intervene; there was a wide variety of weapons around and we had gone through enough shit today for anything else to happen. I had to step in and take control of the situation.

"Stand down! The mission is over; the orders have been successfully completed," Adam replied.

"Regardless of the orders, we had everything under control. You screwed up when you put all of us in harms way," I responded, as I walked a little closer to Adam.

"That was un-cool! We all had our backs to you," Mason added.

"I didn't shoot at Rocco, stop whining! The mission is complete and none of you were hurt. Rocco, go fetch a broom and make this place squeaky clean. We will all meet at Banks' house for debriefing, when the cleanup is concluded," Adam said, giving us all orders.

"Negative! Since our orders were trumped by yours; you can finish up. I am taking Rocco with me. Mason is going to take us to Banks,' I want to see Sarah. Dante please make sure everything is taken care of; you're in charge, feel free to let Adam do all the work."

"What? We're finishing this together; I'm in charge," Adam replied.

"You're not in charge of shit!" Rocco responded.

"Yeah, you should really do what you're told. You are losing allies by the second," Mason added.

"What am I the enemy now?" Adam responded.

"No, just you have lost your title of leader for the time being," Mason replied.

"That's the cost of being trigger happy; we can take it up with Banks tomorrow. None of us are happy with you right now; we're leaving. Dante are you cool? Will you stay?" I said.

"Yeah, as soon as the four of us conclude our business with Ponce, you guys can get out of here; we'll finish up around here." Dante understood; he knew I was right. I felt bad leaving him there. I knew he would do all the work as soon as we were out of sight. We walked over to Ponce and the four of us each shoots him in the chest. That was done so everyone in the room had a hand in killing him. We get in the Hummer and start on our way to Banks,' leaving Dante and Adam to finish the job. They had to clean up and wipe the place down, so that no evidence could be found that any of us were ever there.

Mason and Rocco dropped me off at my apartment to get my car. I handed Rocco my gun and left all my gear when we arrived. They were going to go dispose of the guns along with the gear and clean out the Hummer; leaving no trace of

Ponce that could be found. I went in my apartment and changed clothes; I put the clothes and the boots I wore in a garbage bag and brought it to them waiting outside. We said our goodbyes and they were off. I went back inside and took a shower. I had to be clean before I set foot in Banks' house. I packed a bag and got everything I needed; then I was off.

I arrived at Banks' house; I walked to the door and knocked. At that point, it finally hit me. Banks opened the door and I walked inside. I only went a few feet before he hugged me.

"This day has been crazy. It was awfully convenient that the police went on strike 30 minutes before the bomb exploded," I said.

"Yeah, the F.B.I. is checking into the coincidence as we speak. My sources say that there was no connection with the two. However, it does look bad. It is a good thing we stepped up and we took care of the terrorist ourselves. Thank you for doing it; I appreciate it. Oh, I wish I would have been there to do it myself; but, I had to see my baby girl for myself," Banks responded.

"Banks the adrenaline has worn off and she's gone." Both of our eyes began to tear up. "I am mentally worn down from this day and I can only imagine what tomorrow will be like. I need a vacation. I don't know for how long, but I just need time away from here. To do this job for you, my mind has to be focused and, now, it's not. I don't know when it will be. You can keep tabs on me or whatever you have to do, just let me go." I sincerely and respectfully said.

"I really want you to stay so we can help each other through this; but, I completely understand. Do whatever you have to do and take as long as you need."

"You know I was going ring shopping this week. Now, I don't know what to do," I said, as I fought to hold back tears.

"There is nothing, I would have loved more than to walk my daughter down the isle with you waiting to take her hand. Kastle, I love you like a son. Please, take care of yourself."

"You too. I'll keep in touch. If there is any emergencies, text me or leave a message and I'll get back to you. Well, let me go. I'll see ya. Goodbye!" Then, I was finally off.

Chapter 9
Rehab

Emotionally drained and feeling nothing but pain, I got behind the wheel of my Mercedes. A much needed road trip to an undetermined destination was the only thing on my mind, at that particular moment. I got on the road, but I didn't get too far before I had to make a gas stop. I found a place outside of Jacksonville to fuel up. While I was pumping gas a person approached me.

"Kastle Raines! Oh my God it's so good to see you. I am so sorry." Naomi said, teary eyed, as she gave me a heart felt hug.

"Naomi, I thought you were in the school," I replied. I was completely shocked to see her. Naomi was also a teacher at the school.

"My father had surgery in Orlando yesterday. I am just getting back. All of this is unbelievable. I have been trying to call Sarah and her dad all day long to find out if she was okay. I finally got a hold of him about an hour ago and he gave me the bad news. I have been crying all day."

"I know; this is a nightmare."

"Where are you going?" Naomi asked.

"I really don't know. I just need to get away."

"Oh, I'm sure. Look, if you ever want to talk, I am here for you. Here is my number; you can call me anytime. I have to run; but, please, don't hesitate to call. It is going to be hard on everyone for a long time; maybe we all can help each other through this."

"Yeah, it's going to be tough. When I get back in town, I'll give you a call. In the mean time, take care of yourself."

"You as well," Naomi said. She gave me a goodbye hug and then we both were on our way. I continued south and I drove all night. I didn't know where I was going, I just drove. The only thing I was sure about was that, I wanted to be alone. When the sun came up, I was feeling fatigued and decided to stop. I grabbed a bottle of Jack and a six pack of beer, and then crashed at a hotel. I felt I would need alcohol to go to sleep; but, a part of me thought that whiskey would not even help. I got to my room and immediately started drinking. I downed one beer and that was it. The exhaustion overwhelmed me; I was out.

The next couple of days were a blur. If I was not sleeping, I was drinking. It was definitely more drinking than sleeping; it just hurt to shut my eyes. I woke up one morning face down in the sand, with an empty bottle in my hand, and the sun beaming down on me. I had no idea how I got there. The sun was just what I needed. After a shower and a bite to eat, the initial shock of the tragedy was over.

I called Banks to ask him about the funeral arrangements. He told me her body was in too bad of shape to show, so he had it cremated. I told him that I could not go back at that time, and couldn't go to the funeral. At the time, it felt meaningless to go and say goodbye to an urn; I couldn't do it. He said he understood and supported whatever I did. Also, he let me know that the apartment situation was taken care of. He moved me out, and had all of my belongings put into storage. I had to get a new place when I returned; it would have been way too hard to live there.

I continued struggling over Sarah's death. My thoughts were all about her; and if there was a moment that I did not think of her, the flashback of me killing a man would enter my mind. Even though Adam actually killed him with the first shot, I saw him die. I believed that he deserved it, but it was still hard to handle. It was the first time I had witnessed anyone's death. It was definitely a tough couple of weeks. Sarah was the first woman that I ever really loved. I could not see the never-ending agony, I was enduring, ever going away.

During the first month, I stayed in hotels up and down the Florida coastline; eventually, landing in Miami. I was there for about a week, before I felt that it was best to get out of Florida and travel. It took that long for me to want to be around anyone. I did not want my Mercedes anymore; so, I traded it in on a Range Rover. They had to special order it; so, it would be at least a week before it would be in. I did not care. I just wanted out of that car. I did not want to worry about anything when I was traveling, especially a car that I did not even want. So, that is why I traded it in before I left, and I really wanted a new car. A cab brought me to the hotel and then to the airport.

I flew home to see my parents in California. I stayed with them a few days, while I contemplated on where to go and what to do. My mom and dad were a big help. They knew how much I loved Sarah, even though they never got the chance to meet her.

After I spent some time with the parents, I went to L.A. to meet up with Tristan. I met him at the Coffee Ville on Sunset Blvd.; he was already there when I arrived.

"Kastle, it is so good to see you," Tristan said, as we greet each other with a hand shake and then a hug.

"It's good to see you too. Thanks for meeting me," I replied.

"I'm glad you called. What are you doing here? Have you come to take me up on my job offer?"

"I'm just taking a little vacation; I visited my parents for a few days and thought while I was here I would see what you were doing," I responded.

"I'm glad you did. I tried to call you a couple of weeks ago when I was in Jacksonville. Sophie and I were there doing a fundraiser for the school that was blown up."

"Yeah I got your call, but I couldn't talk at the time. My girlfriend was a teacher at that school," I replied.

"Jesus! Bro, I'm so sorry. I had no idea. I wish I would have known; that was so unbelievably tragic. How have you been doing?" Tristan sincerely said.

"It has been rough, but I've gradually been getting better."

"Now I know what you meant when you said vacation. Today you're going to hang with me. Sophie is in New York; I know exactly what we can do. Let me make a few calls. I'll be right back," Tristan replied.

"That sounds good. I don't have any plans." Tristan walks away from the table and returns a few minutes later.

"I have everything all set up. Tonight, we've got floor seats for the Laker Game. I have a meeting with my agent; I have to go to, for a few hours. I've arranged for you to be well taken care of, while I'm there," Tristan said.

"A hooker is not necessary. I just want to take it easy a few days," I replied.

"Come on, trust me! I know what need! You are going to get an old school barber shop shave; then, you're on to the spa. You will get one of the best massages, ever, along with a happy ending; that's only if you want it. I'll pick you up there;

then, we'll get to the other items we have on our agenda," Tristan said, as he dropped me off at the barber shop on his way to his meeting. His driver later returned to bring me to the spa. After the greatest massage ever, I rejoined Tristan, anxious to see what else he had planned. We went to see his personal stylist; we both got haircuts and then we went shopping for clothes to wear to the game. On the way there, I noticed a car tailing us; I thought it was probably just a fan or the paparazzi. When we finished shopping; we walked back to the car and I spotted the same car parked four spaces behind us.

"Do you have somebody you can call to get information on a license plate?" I asked Tristan, when we were a couple of feet from the car.

"Yeah, one of my bodyguards has a brother who's a cop; he can find out anything I need. Why? What's up?" Tristan said, as we stood in front of his car.

"Don't look, but the grey Tahoe over there has been following us all day." We get in Tristan's Escalade and went to a coffee shop, four blocks down the street. The guy in the Tahoe continued to follow us.

"He's probably some tabloid reporter trying to find out who the hell you are," Tristan replied, with a logical explanation.

"Maybe. I would feel better if we get confirmation that what you are saying is true," I responded.

"Okay Riley, drop us off at Coffee Ville and then park. Jason, get his plate number and see what your brother can find out." Tristan sends his guys to go get what I want, while we go into the coffee shop and act like nothing is going on. We just ordered a coffee and talked. I had a hunch why the guy was following us, but I didn't say anything.

"How did your meeting go?" I asked Tristan, while we were sitting at a table waiting for his guys.

"It went great. How did the massage go?" Tristan said.

"It was amazing; especially the ending," I answered.

"I told you Kastle; I know what I'm talking about. In fact, you should listen to me more often and come and work for me. My next movie will be back in Miami. You could be head of security for me. This job is yours if you want it; just think about it. I would love to have you around. Plus, I would feel much safer."

"I'll think about it. What else did you do besides the meeting?"

"My production company is shooting a few scenes this afternoon; so, I had to make sure everything was ready to go. You know they're shooting not too far from here, if you want to check it out. We have some time before we have to be at the game." Jason comes in and tells us what his brother had found out.

"The Tahoe is a rental and it was paid for by RB Security Company located in Jacksonville."

"It's okay. Tell your brother, I appreciate the info. Let me talk to Kastle; we'll be out in a few minutes. Now, why is your company having us followed?"

"My boss just wants to make sure I'm alright. I told him I needed to take some time off and I didn't tell him where I was going or when I was coming back; he was worried about me. He just lost his daughter, my girlfriend; and doesn't want to lose anybody else," I said, as I explained the situation.

"Okay, I understand. So what now? He's going to follow us wherever we go," Tristan said to me.

"Yeah, it's another person that has our back; there's nothing wrong with extra security. What scene are they shooting on the movie you were talking about earlier?" I asked.

"They're doing a fight scene in the middle of a street. Why? Do you want to go?" Tristan replied, after he took a sip of coffee.

"Maybe. We do have some time to kill," I replied.

"The fight scene choreographer is brilliant; it should be a kick ass scene," Tristan said, as he took another sip of his coffee and I did as well.

"You know what, I have an idea. Do you think the director could use another extra?" I said with a smile.

"I like it! I'll call and set it up." Tristan knew exactly what I had in mind. He called the director and discussed our plan. The director was really excited; he thought this would provide a sense of realism to the scene. He told Tristan what time to be there. We finished our coffee and headed over to the set.

When we left Coffee Ville, the Tahoe continued to tail us, everything was going as planned. Tristan stayed on the phone with the director, while we were in transit, to make sure everything went smoothly. Every so often, he turned around to make sure the guy was still following us. He was really enjoying this; actually, we all were. As we got closer, they unblocked the streets so the guy in the Tahoe, who continued to tail us, would not be suspicious. As we drove down the street everything looked normal. When we turned the corner, I could see the fight going on behind us. The plan was to have us lead the Tahoe down the street and an actor would run out in front of the car that was in front of the Tahoe and the fight would be going on in front of and all around the Tahoe. The director said that Banks' guy would be blocked in for at least an hour. I would have loved to have been there to see his face when a couple of guys jumped out in front of a car and begin to fight right in front of him. They had stunt men being thrown on top of cars and even their heads going thru windows; it sounded pretty amazing. It went even better than I imagined; but, then again, in Hollywood, it's supposed to. Tristan said he would get me a copy of the scene as soon as he could.

We went to Tristan's house and started to get ready for the game. The Laker game is always a big event in L.A.; the who's who of Hollywood is always in attendance. With the tabloids surely to focus on the absence of Sophie with Tristan, he had to give his publicist and Sophie the heads up. Sophie was okay with it and sent her condolences to me; his publicist, on the other hand, wasn't too happy. She new her phone would be ringing off the hook for the next week or two, because her movie star client was without his lady friend.

We arrived at the game early; I didn't want to miss the starting lineup introductions or any of the game. I was really pumped up for the incredible match up of two great teams; the L.A. Lakers and the Miami Heat. Around the arena there were a number of celebrities there; ranging anywhere from the music industry to politics. Once we made it to our seats we found a celebrity sitting in the seat right next to Tristan; a hip hop artist from Miami, Rushon Little.

"Rush let me introduce you to a good friend of mine, Kastle Raines. Rush is doing a concert here tomorrow night and he's a Miami Heat fan," Tristan said.

"I'm a huge Heat fan! It's nice to meet you," Rush tells me, as he reaches over to shake my hand.

"It's a pleasure to meet you! I'm a big fan. I love your music," I responded.

"Kastle works for a security company in Jacksonville," Tristan added.

"Jacksonville, huh, I hated to see that happen again. I hope they find that Arkbar Rahad and give the bastard what he deserves; jail will be too good for him. Al Qaeda is still fucking with us. We should have taken them out after 9-11. It was a huge tragedy; it gets me pissed every time I think about it," Rush said.

"Yeah, I hope they find him too," I responded. I was still pretty shocked that Ponce was not believed to be responsible for the bombing. I had been in my own world, so I had not watched any news or radio. Thus, that was the first time that I had heard of it.

"Let me know if you need any tickets, back stage passes, or anything; just give me a number and I got you. Kaz, you too. Any friend of my dog right here, is cool with me," Rush said, as he gave Tristan a fist bump.

"We appreciate it Rush; I might have to take you up on that. In a few weeks, I will be in Miami working. You know, there are a couple of roles you would be ideal for. That is if you are available, and if you can act," Tristan replied.

"Oh, I can act! I have many skills cuz. Yeah, you need to hook that up. The tour wraps up next weekend; I'm doing my last show in Miami," Rush responded.

"I'll put in a good word for you; just don't let me down," Tristan said to Rush.

"Success is all I know, movie star, trust me..." Rush continued talking. I couldn't hear him for the starting lineup introductions; he was sitting on the other side of Tristan. I enjoyed the introductions; the music really gets you pumped up. It was a close game until the Lakers pulled away in the fourth quarter. I was a little disappointed though because, I wanted to see a last second shot to win the game or at least a closer game than it turned out to be. Altogether, I cannot complain. Being the big sports fan I am, I had a ball. It was just what I needed.

After the game, Tristan clued me in on our next destination: Vegas. We didn't get there until sometime after 3 A.M.; then again, time doesn't matter there. You lose track of time; twelve hours will go by before you know it. It is a great place to go to lose yourself and not think about anything in the world during the few hours that you are there. On the other hand, you can also lose a lot of money. I love to gamble; yet, I am very tight with my money. I refuse to lose large amounts of my hard earned cash; unlike, my buddy, Tristan. I saw him lose up to fifty grand, on one hand, of blackjack. Although, I think he was surprised with the amount I was gambling with. We hit the tables and played for hours that night. Blackjack, craps, and roulette were the games we played the majority of the time; but, we tried everything. If we went on a cold streak on one table, we would move on to the next. To play as long as we did, our system worked out pretty good. After taking care of the dealers and wait staff, I left with $20,000 and Tristan ended up with $50,000; it was a great night. After five hours of gambling, we crashed in our suites before going back to L.A later that night.

When we arrived, I accepted Tristan's offer of being in charge of his security. I told him I was his, while he was in Miami; but, I had to think about anything further. He was pleased with my decision and said he would see me in three weeks. I, then, headed to the airport to catch my flight back to Miami. Once I arrived, I didn't want to go back yet; I had another destination in mind.

It was a long flight to New York, but it was something I had to do. Before I left the airport, I had to pick up an umbrella; it was pouring the entire time I was there. I only stayed a few hours; but, there was one place, I just had to see. I caught a cab and went to lower Manhattan to visit what used to be the World Trade Center. I walked around the outside of the construction site in the rain holding an umbrella, imagining what it was like that tragic day. I remember the images I saw on the news reports and I stood there visioning the events as they had occurred. I felt the same as I did that day in Jacksonville; even though, I didn't know anyone involved, the hurt was the same. I reflected on everything that had happened in the last year and on the recent information about Arkbar Rahad, that I received from Rush.

After visiting a tragic part of American history, I had a meal at the first café I came too and then returned to the airport to catch another flight. My next stop was Jacksonville, before I returned to Miami.

I arrived in Jacksonville, immediately, catching a cab to the school. It was the first time I had been there in person, since the explosion had occurred. I stood there on the sidewalk painfully looking at what was left of the building on, what was now, a construction site. All I could think about was Sarah and all of the children who lost their young lives there or who were traumatized from that tragic event. It truly was heartbreaking to just think about. I was there only for a couple of minutes, when I heard someone approaching behind me.

"What took you so long? I thought you would have been waiting for me when I got off the plane," I said, while I continued to look strait forward.

"I thought you were on your way to see me. How was New York?" Banks asked, as he walked up and stood beside me, instantly shaking my hand and then giving me a hug. "It is so good to see you."

"I see your guy has improved his tailing skills. It's good to see you too," I replied at the conclusion of our man hug.

"That stunt you pulled on my new guy was pretty funny."

"We were bored; so, I just had to mess with him. You have to admit that it was pretty creative and he will have a great story to tell. I left a trail for him to find me again. I knew he was watching my back for you. That's the only reason the rental car was traced back to you, right."

"I have taught you well. So, what's next? Are you ready to come back?" Banks said, with a big smile on his face.

"Not yet, I have to be 100 percent ready to come back. I have some more issues to sort through. I am going to ease my way back into everything; which is why I am here. I am going to be head of Tristan's security while he is in Miami shooting his next movie. I'm hoping everything will be all good in a couple months and I'll be back here ready to work."

"I understand. You know, you could have told me this over the phone," Banks responded.

"Yeah, but I had to know if Ponce really was responsible for the bombing. Why were we the only ones looking for him? The F.B.I. and everyone else were looking for this Arkbar Rahad? It's pretty close to arm bar rawhide; come on, it sounds like someone had to think of something quick and made it up."

"We received Intel from a reliable source that Ponce was responsible. Al Qaeda immediately took credit for it and released Arkbar as the bomber. No one knows anything about the Cottos; there is a lot that is unknown. We're trying to find out why it happened and where they are; we will find them," Banks replied.

"So, no one knows about Ponce?" I asked again, to make sure that we were in the clear.

"No one is asking or looking for him; they are looking for Arkbar. We are in the clear. We took care of the man responsible! You can relax, there is nothing to worry about; but, if something comes up we will let you know. Just go to Miami and try to enjoy yourself. When you're ready to come back, we'll be glad to see you."

"There is something else. There has to be something we can do to prevent anything like the school bombing for ever happening again. You have contacts and all of the Intel that we would need," I said.

"America has the greatest military in the world and various agencies to take care of all of that. I know you want to do more, but we have done our part; we disposed of a terrorist. We all need to move on with our lives; it will be hard, but that is what Sarah would want for all of us. Now, for me, will you try and do that?" Banks said.

"I will try."

"That's good to hear. Well, I have to go. I'll see you. Take care of yourself and call me if you need anything."

"I'll see you, Banks." Banks walked off, while I continued to look at Ponce's work. Even though it was nothing like what it was, I saw the images I observed from Banks' Plasma. I stayed there a few minutes and then returned to the airport. A couple hours later, I finally made it back to Miami. I got a cab and went to a hotel and crashed; the jet lag had finally caught up with me.

I rolled out of bed the next morning, with a big day ahead of me. I had many things to get accomplished; I had to get a car and find a place to live. I had a few weeks before Tristan would be arriving, so I had some time to find an apartment. Even though hotel rooms were getting old, I could deal with it for the time being. I began the day by picking up my new, black Range Rover that I had ordered before my trip to California. It was exactly what I wanted. When I left the dealership, I checked out a few places around the location of the house that Tristan would be renting. I decided on one, and began to move in that day. I bought a bed and saved the rest of the furniture buying for the next couple of days. I just had to get off that hotel mattress and back to my life.

Chapter 10
Snapshots over Fisticuffs

In the next two weeks, I spent my time acquiring the essentials; a plasma TV, a DVD player, computer, and other necessities. Then, I had to buy clothes; my wardrobe needed to be severely updated and well-stocked. When I wasn't shopping, I was working out. I had to get myself back in shape. I had been slipping the last month. I was set back from the drinking, smoking, a short stint with depression, and just being plain lazy. I wanted to be on my A game when I went to work; although the head of Tristan's security is more like a figure head position. Really, it was absolutely what I needed. It gave me time to contemplate my future and regain my sharpness, if I decided to continue in this line of work. In the back of my mind I knew what I wanted, but at the time it seemed impractical.

Tristan arrived in Miami a few days before shooting started on his movie; which gave me some time to meet his security guys and let me see what I had to work with. They seemed to know what they were doing, so I was just an extra pair of eyes. I watched over them and stayed out of their way, for the most part. However, I did make it clear that I had the final say in all situations that came up.

One week had passed and everything was going smoothly. All of us were in a routine. Tristan was taking care of the acting and we were taking care of him. He was working long hours that first week; so, the set was the only place he went. Our job during the week was rather easy.

Sophie came down on that Friday night, since he was off for the rest of the weekend. They met at a club to enjoy some well deserved drinks for a long and hard week. We welcomed the change of scenery. When Tristan and the rest of us arrived at the classy place, we found Sophie sitting at a table with Bianca and some guy. Bianca was in town doing a photo shoot and the guy was trying to get lucky I'm sure. When we first reached the table Tristan introduced me to the guy, while Bianca and I barely spoke; although, she did give me a "hello." The guy she was with was someone she worked with; Tristan said his name when he introduced us, but I didn't catch it. I had a five second lapse after seeing Bianca. However, I did hear the part about them working with each other. I was shocked to see her. Plus, she looked extremely hot; even better than I remembered. Her co-worker gave me a look of irrelevance, which didn't bother me. It was the first time the guy had met Tristan; he was star struck. Unless the President was standing there, anyone would have been seen to be insignificant. I only hung around the table for a few minutes. In that short time, I got to witness Bianca's guy kiss some serious ass, along with ignoring his beautiful date. This was, very obviously, making her very annoyed.

"Oh, did you bring it?" Tristan asked Sophie. She, then, reached into her designer handbag.

"Yes, I did," Sophie replied, as she gave Tristan a relatively small box.

"I love your bag," Bianca said.

"It's a Coach. Tristan got it for me," Sophie replied.

"I haven't seen that one before, is it even available yet?" Bianca asked.

"I don't think so; but I'll talk Tristan into getting you one." Sophie replied, as she slowly caressed his hand.

"I'll see what I can do," Tristan said, as he approaches me and pulls me to the side.

"I have a little something for you; just to show my appreciation for you working for me," Tristan said, as he handed the box to me.

"Thank you," I replied, as I opened the gift and found an Omega Deville Watch.

"I saw that you already had the Sea master. I hope you like it?" Tristan said.

"I love it! Thank you," I said, after I was momentarily flustered with my gift. It was exactly like the watch that Ponce was wearing, when I last saw him. I continued to observe everything that was going on in the area. As much as I tried to fight it, my attention always returned to Bianca. It was obvious that my mind wasn't on my job; so, I felt I needed to regroup and concentrate on the job at hand. I went to the bar to get a drink and to get away; watching the pathetic actions of Bianca's date was disturbing, I needed alcohol. Actually, her date wasn't that bad; I was just a little bitter. I could not believe that she was with him. The only time that I was around Bianca I felt something, but I couldn't explore it.

I continued standing with my back to the bar; consuming my drink and maintaining a clear view of their table. I, normally, would not drink on duty; but, my job description was different. I was not directly guarding the client and I was not going to get drunk. I was there more as a friend of Tristan's, than anything else. The job was getting done; I always made sure of it. Tristan wanted me to have a good time, but be somewhat alert. Tristan said he just felt better having me around, in any capacity. I maintained a continuous watch on the table; it even looked boring from where I was standing. I surveyed their immediate surroundings and then began scanning the entire room looking for anything out of the ordinary. While observing everyone in the area, I noticed two hot brunettes wearing skin tight short dresses. They walked up to the bar and stood next to me, while patiently waiting for the bartender. I noticed the one closest to me taking a cigarette out of her pack. I, immediately, turn to my right; now, with my entire body now facing the bar, I light her cigarette with the lighter that I normally carry in my pocket.

"Thank you!" The girl said, in a cute party girl voice. She started to say something else, but I had to interrupt her.

"You are welcome. Excuse me," I replied, as I immediately turned around just as Bianca reached the bar; now standing next to me.

"Hi!" Bianca said.

"Hello!" I replied.

"I didn't know you smoked?" Bianca asked, as she sat her drink down on the bar.

"I don't. I just like to get the attention of gorgeous women, so I can lure them away from their boring dates. Come with me. Let's get lost in a crowd," I said, as I grabbed Bianca's hand and walked toward the dance floor with her walking close behind. I was working, so my client's best interest always came first. Rolling around on the floor of a club with some jealous dude, would not be good for my high profile boss. We reached the outskirts of the dance floor and could not go any further. The whole place was packed; it was a tight squeeze where we were. I stopped and turned around; our bodies were extremely close and we were face to face. We stood there with everyone around us moving and dancing to the music. We looked in to each others eyes and just got lost; the entire world was moving around us and we stood still. I leaned towards Bianca slowly; I was caught up in the moment and went for it. Right before my lips made it to hers, she put her hands on my chest and stopped me. She stood there not saying anything. While leaving her left hand on my chest, she took her right hand off and put her index and middle fingers up to her lips. She stuck out her tongue just enough to touch her fingers, and then placed her fingers on my chest touching my shirt. She gently grasps a hold of my shirt with her left hand, while she leans in and gets close to my left ear and speaks with her sexy voice.

"You are all wet, let's get you out of these wet clothes." I was speechless at first; there was only one thing I could think of.

"Let's get out of here." There wasn't much dialogue in our little moment, but it was amazing. We made our way slowly through the crowd and finally reached a point where we could see Tristan and Sophie. Before we made it to them, to tell them we were leaving; we were stopped in our tracks.

"I've been looking for you. I could have walked you to the restroom, you didn't need the bodyguard. Thank you for your services, although unnecessary; but, I can handle everything from here. Hey babe, let's go cut a rug." The entire time he was talking I stood there not saying a word. I kept my composure. I couldn't blame the guy for feeling like he was on top of the world, with a hot date by his side and hanging out with movie stars and all. I held my tongue for the time being. Although he was, definitely, only one annoying comment away from surpassing my limit of verbal abuse.

"Look, we have to talk. Thank you for coming with me tonight. I hate to leave so early, especially since I asked you to come here. What can

I say, just bad timing. Actually, for once it's good timing for me." Bianca glances at me and smiles, when she says the good timing part.

"You're leaving with the help?" The guy said to Bianca.

"The help!" I replied in astonishment, as I took two steps towards them. Tristan, Sophie, and their security walked up just as I spoke.

"I asked you to join me and a couple of friends for drinks, not to go on a date. I didn't know Kastle would be here or I wouldn't have invited you. I am sorry if I mislead you in any way; I hope you have a good time for the rest of the night." Bianca sincerely apologized for the whole situation and her early exit.

"I'm disappointed, but I understand. You can stay for a couple more drinks can't you?" Her coworker said.

"No, thank you. We're leaving," Bianca replied, with a noticeable amount of aggravation in her voice.

"What, you two are leaving? When did this happen?" Sophie asked with complete surprise. However, she did have a satisfying grin on her beautiful face.

"Yeah, you can have a few more, it is still early. Your bodyguard here can earn his money and go watch the table for us while we go dance… as friends of course." The guy said, with a smart ass grin on his face, as he reached out to grab Bianca's hand. I, immediately, grabbed his shoulders and pulled him backwards and handed him off to the two bodyguards.

"Take him to the bouncers and make sure he is eighty-sixed. He has had a few too many." What I really wanted to do was slam him to the floor and pound on his face, but I didn't. At the time, leaving with Bianca was definitely more appealing.

"Kastle, I told you that you and Bianca would be perfect together. Can I get a thank you Sophie?" Sophie said.

"Thank you Sophie. We're going to cut out of here; you guys are in very good hands," I acknowledged to Tristan and Sophie.

"You are too. We'll see you two tomorrow," Tristan replied, as we said our goodbyes to the both of them. We waited there until their security returned before we finally exited. I grabbed her hand and quickly escorted her outside the club. The rain outside was coming down pretty good. Anxious to leave, we just took off running to Bianca's car. She was leading the way since she knew where she parked and I had never seen her car.

"Which one is yours?" I said, as I was jogging beside her.

"It's the white BMW over there!" Bianca yelled out and pointed to her car. At this point we are still holding hands and running on the sidewalk, until I suddenly stopped.

"I can't wait any longer!" I said, as I pulled her to me and we engaged in a long passionate kiss with a steady stream of raindrops continuing to fall.

"We have to get out of the rain!" Bianca said, as it began to rain a little harder.

"At this moment, nothing else matters; only us," I replied, as I kissed her again. Even though we were drenched when we finally made it to her car, it was worth it; it was an incredible breath-taking moment.

"I feel the same way. I am glad we stopped," she replied. The whole night was amazing. In fact, the next three months were amazing. From the first time we met or definitely from the night on the sidewalk we knew how we felt about each other. When I first saw her, I felt something. I was with Sarah, at the time, so I did not investigate my feelings. The second time I saw her, I knew I was positively in love with her.

Chapter 11
Mrs. Raines

After only three and a half months, I asked Bianca to marry me. She began planning for the wedding, but we did not make it to the date that we set. We decided to get married on a beach in Hawaii; it was a spur of the moment type thing. We were vacationing with Tristan and Sophie when we decided to take the plunge. Both of our parents could not make it on short notice and we invited a number of people but they could not come either. My boys were the only ones who could get away; however, Banks and Adam could not make it. The other three were eager to come to Maui; they sounded bored, when I talked to them over the phone. Dante and Mason came alone and Rocco brought Isabella for a little getaway of their own. The four of them were the only guest that we had at our ceremony on the beach. Tristan was my best man and Sophie was Bianca's maid of honor. Bianca had always dreamed of a wedding on a beach by a waterfall; she got her wish and it was amazing. We both would have liked to have our parents there, but once the thought entered our minds we did not want to wait another day.

We had a small reception in the resort bar back at the Four Seasons Hotel in Maui where we were staying. When we first arrived at our reception, everyone came up to greet the new Mr. and Mrs. Raines. Tristan and Sophie were the first to congratulate us; then, Rocco and Isabella followed.

"Congratulations! Here's a little something for you and your beautiful bride," Rocco said, as he presented me with the buste from him and from Banks.

"Thank you so much; we appreciate it," I replied, as I shook his hand.

"Since it is your wedding day, I will just do the hand shake and not the kiss on the cheek," Rocco stated, while he was shaking my hand.

"That's unnecessary; but, a handshake is fine with me," I replied. However, Bianca did receive the traditional two-cheek kiss. Mason and Dante were next and they brought envelopes as well. I gave each one to Bianca without opening them and graciously thanked the guys for their very generous gifts. After we greeted everyone, they went to be seated at a large table in the corner of the room and then it was explanation time for me; according to the beautiful Mrs. Raines. Bianca pulled me aside out of their view and started counting the money in the envelopes.

"Please tell me why we just had a scene from a mafia movie?"

"My beautiful bride should have elaborate gifts on her wedding day, even if we had a small wedding." I explained to her with a smile on my face.

"Bullshit!" Bianca replied.

"It's called the custom of the buste. It's an Italian tradition that takes place at a wedding. It would be disrespectful to Rocco and the others if we didn't accept their gifts."

"A traditional Italian gift would be a few hundred dollars, and even that would be generous; there is enough in here to buy a car. Kastle, there is twenty-five thousand dollars in cash in my hands; it feels like I just married a made man." Bianca had a surprised and worried look on her face, as she spoke to me.

"So you do pay attention to the gangster movies that you watch with me."

"Are you trying to be funny right now?" Bianca replied.

"What can I say; they are very generous with their money. Obviously, they can afford to give us such elaborate gifts. You're making too much out of this."

"Well, maybe. I just have never seen this before."

"Baby, can we accept our wedding gifts from our friends and go enjoy our wedding night?" I asked my beautiful bride. At this point, I have not told her anything about my other money and the other activities that I had done with my friends. That conversation would take place in the future, if ever.

"I do deserve expensive gifts on my wedding day. Okay, I'll let it go. Let's get back to our generous guests."

"Now will you dance with your husband, Mrs. Raines?"

"There is nothing in the world that I want more."

"What do you say one dance and we sneak off, so I can treasure hunt?" I said. Bianca's sleeping habits were somewhat strange. She would have to have her own sheet to herself before she could go to sleep. Her personal sheet would be wrapped around and this definitely hindered any late night activities that arose. To get what I wanted, I had to hunt for it; and let me tell you, it was always rewarding.

"We have all night. I promise it will be well worth the wait. I have been waiting for my wedding night all of my life. You just wait, it will be memorable," Bianca responded. I, then, grabbed her hand and led her to the dance floor to have our first dance as husband and wife. This was the first step in my attempt to give my gorgeous bride her perfect night. We danced, we drank, and we had a wonderful time with our guests. The reception, the wedding night, the entire week we spent in Hawaii, was perfect.

Bianca and I returned to Miami to get back to our jobs and began our lives together. We purchased a new house in a suburb in Miami with some money I had saved. Actually, it was more like a mansion; it was huge. Over the years I had saved the money I made during my baseball career. I only lived in apartments and spent little money. I had a savings account that I did not touch that accumulated a large amount of interest. Well, most of it came from that, but some came from my offshore account that Gus put in there under the radar. After buying the house and fully furnishing it the way we wanted, I still had money in the savings account. Plus, I still had a large amount available in the offshore account.

Bianca started back at work. Luckily enough, Tress Magazine had an office in Miami and they were happy to have her. I had a plan of my own to have a job in Miami; however, I had to talk it over with Banks first. I flew to Jacksonville to run my idea by Banks; I felt like I should talk to him in person. I took a cab from the airport and when I arrived he was waiting at the door.

"Kastle, my boy, it's so good to see you! How are you?"

"I'm great, how are you? You look good," I said.

"I'm okay. How is married life?" Banks asked me. We walked through his house, to the table by the pool on the back patio. We sit down at the table and continued talking.

"It's great!" I said, as Banks gets up and goes to the bar.

"Would you like a beer?"

"Sure!" I replied. Moments later, he returned to the table with two beers.

"Here you go!" Banks said, as he placed my beer on the table.

"Thank you! Cheers!" I said, as we touch bottles.

"Cheers!" Banks replied.

"So what happened to bourbon?" I said, after I turned up my cold brew.

"Bourbon just made me too angry all the time. I had to let it go," Banks answered.

"We wanted to thank you for the buste; we really appreciate it."

"You're very welcome. It was the least I could do, since I couldn't be there in person. It would have been just too damn hard to see; but, don't get me wrong, I am really happy for you and your new bride."

"I totally understand. It would have been hard to see you there without thinking about Sarah and that wouldn't have been fair to Bianca. She deserved my full attention on our wedding day. It is hard not to think about Sarah; especially the way she died. It took some time to get through it, but I got lucky. I found someone that I loved just as much as Sarah; and I couldn't be happier. In fact, that is why I'm here. We will be happy in Miami. It would be too hard on us to come back here with all the history; good and bad. Plus, Bianca's job is there."

"What does she do?"

"She's a photographer for *Tress Magazine*," I replied.

"Wow, that is great. So how can I help you?" Banks asked.

"I think we can help each other. I have to have some kind of job. What would you say about having a RB Security office in Miami? There is a ton of steady business there," I said.

"That's a good idea. I've always wanted to have a branch office down there. The other guys aren't doing anything around here; take one of them with you."

"I'll take Rocco, if he'll move and leave the bachelors here together."

"I'll ask him; but, I don't know if he'll want to leave Adam," Banks sarcastically responded.

"It shouldn't be too hard to cut the cord," I replied, as we both laughed.

"No, it shouldn't," Banks responded while we were laughing.

"I appreciate this. I didn't know what I was going to do if you said no."

"No, thank you; this will be great for business. Although, I have something coming up I want you in on; but, in your newlywed status, I will totally understand if you decline. I will let you and the others know about it soon. I think it will be something you and the boys would be interested in." When he said that, my imagination went wild. I almost said no right then, but I didn't. I decided to hear him out, and to wait to give him an answer when he pitched it to us.

After we finished our meeting, he called Rocco to come over to talk about my proposal and to take me to the airport. He was all for it, but he had to talk to Isabella before he said yes. He sounded pretty excited about it when he drove me to the airport.

Back in Miami, Bianca and I continued to get settled in our new home and our jobs. I spent my time during the day looking for office space for the company. Rocco agreed to run the business in Miami with me; but, he had to sell his house in Jacksonville first. Thus, along with searching for a place for the business, I checked out a few houses for them. I wanted to already have a selection for them to look at, when they came down to house hunt. I tried to be helpful and speed up the whole process, as much as I could. I, also, had various options for me and Rocco to choose from to use for the business.

Chapter 12
Search and Rescue

It was, exactly, three weeks, later when Rocco called me and told me that they sold the house and they were on their way. I remember, because he called me back an hour later and gave me the terrible news that Banks' private jet had just crashed. His jet went down in the Atlantic, approximately twenty miles off the coast, from an explosion. Upon hearing the word "explosion," the words "here we go again" immediately came to mind. Investigators suspected that it was a bomb that caused the explosion; however, law enforcement officials released a statement, after a thorough investigation, revealing electrical problems as the cause of the crash. There was no hard evidence found, with pieces of the jet spread out in the Atlantic, to support the theory of a bomb. The search for Banks' body was ended after three days. The area was severely shark infested which hindered a thorough search. The conclusion was made that his body was eaten by sharks.

I met Rocco, Mason, and Dante in Jacksonville on day three of the search. We rented a helicopter to check out the situation and even then, we observed a number of sharks in a mile radius. Even though it was extremely difficult and almost unbearable, at the end of the day, we accepted that he was gone.

A week after the search ended, Bianca and I attended a memorial service for Banks at a church in Jacksonville. I expected a small gathering of people who worked for him and a few of his friends; but, it had to have been over a hundred people there. It was over whelming to see how well liked and respected he was. As I sat and listened to all the wonderful things that Gus and a number of others had to say about Banks, my mind began to wander. I could not believe how much my life had changed. Two years before, I was chasing a dream and living a pretty regular life. Was this really the path that I was suppose to take and what did I have in store for me in the next two years? Those were some of the questions I asked myself as I sat there. With those questions came a long list of "what ifs." Then, something happened that I took as a sign that everything would be okay. Bianca held my hand and gave me a comforting look. I pulled her hand up and kissed the back of it and returned my attention back to the speaker.

When the service was over most of Banks' closest friends met back at his house, where a catering service had prepared a meal for everyone. Gus met me as soon as we arrived and brought me in to Banks' private office to talk.

"I wanted to talk to you before we meet with the others. I have Banks' will in testament that I want to go over with you. He has given you boys the business. He wanted you and Rocco to run the business in Miami and Mason and Dante to run the Jacksonville office. He gave the house to me and all of his money in his savings account was donated to the rebuilding of the school fund." Gus said, as he sat behind the desk and I sat across from him.

"Wow, I thought Adam would get the business."

"No, Adam didn't get anything! Banks would always look after him; but, they didn't always see eye to eye," Gus responded.

"I bet he's pissed about that. Where is he any way? I didn't see him at the memorial," I said.

"Adam has been off the grid for weeks now; no one can find him," Gus replied.

"What! That's hard to believe," I responded

"Believe it! I have a lot of sources and they all have come up empty. The only explanation we can gather is that he has been taken out just like Banks," Gus explained.

"So, the Cotto brothers are behind all of this?" I asked.

"That is what it is adding up to look like. Adam goes missing for two weeks then Banks is blown out of the sky. It appears that they got to

Adam and he gave up Banks. If that's the case, it is guaranteed that we all are on their list. That brings me to Banks' offshore accounts and his other wishes." Gus then walked over to a safe that was behind the desk and opened it.

"I forgot about all of that. There must be a ton offshore," I replied.

"There is and it is all set aside for the plan that is explained in these folders," Gus said, as he takes a folder out of the safe and places it in my hands. I looked down and saw my name and the title of the folder, Operation K5, in black letters.

"The last time I saw him, he told me that he was working on something for us and I guess this is it," I said. I, then, opened the folder and commenced to read the first typed page as Gus began to talk.

"Yes, you are right. After your trip to New York, when Banks met with you, he began to put his plan together. We received Intel that the school bombing was the first of many planned terrorist attacks. The Cotto brothers are the key to the operation; if not behind everything. Banks' plan, the one you have in your hands, is to stop these attacks from happening. You guys would be a helping hand to the military and all the government agencies. The group would be funded by the hefty amount of money that is in the offshore account that Banks had stashed away. It is dangerous and you guys could go to jail for this; that is, if you get caught. Which, I think we are all too intelligent and too well trained to let that happen. However, he was going to give each of you a choice to do this or not. Now, since they have gotten to Adam and who knows what he told them, the only choice you guys have is to get them first. Think of our families and the lives of innocent Americans we could save if we do this."

"So, you're going to get your hands dirty with us?" I asked with a smile.

"No, I will point you in the right direction; but, I'll have your back preferably from a far distance away," Gus responded, as I continued to look through all of the papers that were in the folder; there were four total.

"Well, this might be our only option," I replied.

"What's all in there?"

"What, you haven't seen all of this?" I asked as, I stopped reading and looked up at him.

"No, it was for your eyes only. In Banks' will, he left me a key to a safety deposit box; in which had the safe's combination along with instructions to give you and the other guys these folders. I knew of his plan; but, I did not know that there were any folders," Gus said.

"It says just about everything you said; more or less. Okay, I'm in. I'll talk to the others; it shouldn't be too hard to get them on board. We'll stop the ones who are responsible for Banks and Sarah's death. Anything further than that will have to be decided when this is over and we all will sit down and discuss it," I replied.

"Well, let's get to it and go find the boys. Time is of the essence," Gus said, with an understandable sense of urgency, as he grabbed three folders from the safe and walked out of the room. I closed the folder after I finished reading the third page. I exited the office, following closely behind Gus. We found Rocco with Isabella and Bianca in the living room. I went to get Rocco and say hello to the girls; while Gus searched for the other two, so we could meet out back to have our private discussion. I walked up to Bianca and put my arm around her, while she was talking to Isabella and Rocco.

"Hey sweetheart. How are you doing? Hey Isabella; Rocco."

"Hey babe, is everything okay?" Bianca asked.

"Yes, everything is fine; we were just discussing the business," I replied.

"What did Gus have to say?" Rocco asked, as he stepped towards me.

"You'll see. We have to meet him and the guys out back for a sit down," I responded

"Do you want me to get you something to eat? You haven't eaten anything all day," Bianca said always looking out for me.

"I'll grab some appetizers to take with me. Are you going to stick around? We might be a while." I said to Bianca.

"You can come with me and Rocco can ride with Kastle when they get through with their meeting. But, you boys come straight home afterwards," Isabella said, as she was starring at Rocco.

"Oh, we have already made plans to go to a strip club with the boys," I replied.

"I can't think of a better way to use 'the buste' for," Rocco said.

"Whatever, just get there in time to take us to dinner. We are going to eat sushi tonight, so don't be late."

"Ladies, we'll see you later. Rocco, let's go. Bye sweetie; see you soon," I said, as I hugged Bianca and gave her a goodbye kiss. Rocco and I said our goodbyes and went to the food table and picked up some appetizers before heading outside. After stopping at the bar to get bottled water, we headed to the pool house.

"These crab cakes are great; you should try some," I proclaimed to Rocco after I ate one.

"I had a big plate of lasagna earlier that was good, but it was nothing like lasagna from the old country." Rocco replied, as we reached the pool house with Gus, Mason, and Dante waiting for us inside.

"Hey boys. Let's get started," Gus said, as he began to hand out the folders with everyone's name on it. Rocco and the guys started reading the contents of their folders, while I picked up where I left off on page four. After I finished the fourth page, I came across another document that contained interesting information on it. The more I examined the information, the more I could not believe what I was reading. I looked in Rocco's folder to see if he had the same paper in his, and he did not. The way Gus was talking earlier, he did not know that the paper was in my folder. The information I found was just too big, I had to think for a second before I revealed the information that I discovered.

"What do you guys say? Let's find the people who killed Banks, Adam, and who are coming for us. As for the anti-terrorism team, we can wait to decide on that. We have families and our own asses to worry about at the moment. So, what do you think?" I said to get the conversation started.

"I'm in! We have to protect our family," Rocco emphatically answered.

"I'm with you, Kastle," Mason replied.

"We're all with you," Dante stated.

"You guys are more experienced in the terminating department; but, when it comes to protecting my family, I will do anything. I think of you fellas as family. I swear, I will have your back under any circumstance; you can count on me," I sincerely declared to the team.

"Kastle, I have had many well decorated soldiers stand beside me and I'm sure I speak for the all of us when I say there is no one I would rather have alongside me. Plus, when it comes to the experienced part; you have as many kills as we do," Dante replied.

"Bullshit!" I shockingly responded.

"No, it's true. We all have been on missions in combat zones, but we never killed anybody. Adam had a few more kills than we do, but not that many. Banks on the other hand had many; he was a sniper for years long before any of us ever met him," Mason replied.

"It's true, I was Banks' spotter. From the first time he pulled the trigger until the last, I was there all of the way. That experience that we went through was one of the main reasons why we became so close," Gus added.

"Gus, we would be honored if you would now spot for us; tell us where to start?" I said, as I turned and faced Gus.

"It would be my pleasure. Banks and Adam only dealt with Ponce in the past, so we don't know much about the other Cotto brothers. Ponce was the only one who ever set foot in Florida; to my knowledge, no one has ever seen the other Cottos before. There might be a slim chance that Adam may have, but he's MIA." Gus replied.

"So we have no clue of their identity. They could be working with the catering service, serving our food and we wouldn't know it." I said, in response to the frustrating reality that our lack of information could result in grave danger for all of us.

"I do have a photo that is said to be them, but is yet to be confirmed. I will send it to you as soon as I get to my computer. Maybe you guys will have some luck in getting confirmation," Gus said in reference to the photos.

"Do you have any idea where would be the best place to start?" Dante asked.

"I've heard that they spend most of their time somewhere around the Virgin Islands and the eastern coast of South America. I will keep on attempting to get a location on these guys from my contacts; you boys should do the same," Gus replied.

"We'll run with it and we'll get it; we have to," Mason said.

"Ponce did a lot of business in Miami, talk to the people he came into contact with. There has to be someone who knows something." Gus told us what he had on the Cottos, which wasn't that much. My rolodex did not contain the list of contacts that Gus was referring too. However, I did have a long shot in mind. The only person I could think of, that may know something, was Rushon Little. On the day I first saw Adam with Ponce, Tristan told me that Rush once ran drugs for Ponce; he might know something about the rest of them. Before I even had a chance to tell the guys of my potential lead my cell phone started to ring. I looked on the caller's i.d. and it was Bianca.

"Excuse me, I've got to take this; I'll only be a second."

"You just saw her, could you be more whipped!" Rocco said with a smile, as I got up from the table.

"If it was Isabella you would be doing the same; only you would've been moving a lot faster," Mason replied, as I walked out by the pool, closing the door behind me.

"Hey baby, what's up?" I said, when I answered the phone.

"Listen! There is a guy here with me and Isabella that says he is a friend of yours," Bianca replied, setting off an instantaneous alarm in my head.

"What? My friends are five feet away from me."

"We are okay. He says he wants to talk to you. He doesn't want to talk on the phone and I can't say his name. Isabella knows him, but I have never seen him before," Bianca said, in a rather calm voice.

"Where are you? Tell me everything that you can without putting you two in any danger," I said while trying to remain calm and poised. My hand had began to shake from the anger I was experiencing.

"We are in Isabella's car. He wants you to meet us at the last place you saw him; and he says if you still don't know who it is, he will give 5 G's to the first one there." The phone was immediately hung up after Bianca stopped talking. Instantly, I hurried back in the pool house to get the others and let them know what was going on.

"Adam is alive, we have to go! He is with Bianca and Isabella," I said, as I opened the door and rushed inside.

"What did he say?" Gus asked, with a look of surprise on his face.

"I only talked to Bianca; he didn't want to talk over the phone or even say his name. He had Bianca to tell me to meet them at the last place I saw him and he had 5 G's for the first one there," I responded.

"He couldn't have just text you? Kastle, I don't like this at all. I don't trust this cocksucker! He could have the Cotto brothers and a small army waiting for us, for all we know; and he has our wives. He should be shot on sight just for that," Rocco angrily replied.

"No, he's smart, a text or an email can come from anybody. A phone call from someone you trust shows us he's using his head and the message is really coming from him," Gus said.

"Adam has been your and Banks's personal fluffer for years; he can do no wrong," Rocco replied.

"I know you are upset; so, I won't take offense to that," Gus responded.

"I'm sorry. I am upset," Rocco said.

"I have never been too fond of Adam; but he is a smart kid and there is a chance that everything is okay," Gus said.

"I have had Adam's blood on my hands and it was a dark red. I don't trust him," I said.

"I saw it too and there was no white or blue; if there ever was," Mason added.

"I don't know about his blood, but Gus he is a lying rat cocksucker. Our wives could be gagged and tied up when we get there. That's if, we don't get shot by his buddies waiting in the shadows," Rocco responded with some valid points.

"He's not the brightest guy we know; it's possible that he has some help," Dante said, making an excellent point of his own.

"He has had a few weeks to plan this out," Mason added.

"I hear what you all are saying, but we are talking about Bianca and Isabella. We have to do something, quick. Rocco; let's go get our wives and have a little talk with Adam," I replied.

"More like a long over due kneecapping for that asshole. What are we waiting on? Let's go!" Rocco responded.

"Gus, will phone you from the road? Let's go boys," I said, as we all exited the pool house.

Chapter 13
Locked and Loaded

The search for our wives was on! We quickly made our way to the driveway and loaded up in Dante's Suburban. Gus manned his usual post at his work station in the basement of Banks' house. There was a hidden room down there that they called their command center. It contained all of the computers and their high tech equipment. We stopped off at a private storage building to pick up some firepower from the team's arsenal. Then, we were off to the warehouse for our, well anticipated, chat with Adam. It was the same warehouse where we took care of Ponce and the last place I saw Adam.

As we approached the warehouse, we decided it was best to park a couple blocks away; so we wouldn't be ambushed if it was a trap. We bailed out of the SUV and grabbed all of our gear out of the back.

"What is this?" I asked, pointing at a bullet proof vest that I had never seen before.

"It's called Dragon Skin Body Armor; with that on you can fall on a grenade and not even get a bruise. They take bulletproof to a whole new level. I had to acquire a few for us," Mason replied, as he handed each of us one.

"Good looking out. I heard about these vests; they are unbelievable," Dante added, as Mason reached in the back of the Suburban and came out with another black bag.

"Here, I have a radio ear piece for each of us; let's test them out," Mason said, as he passed out the communication devices.

"Alpha check!" Dante said, in order to test his microphone and our ear pieces. We followed his lead and continued with the communications trial run.

"Bravo check!" Mason said.

"Charlie check! Rocco said.

"K check!" I said, because I had no idea what the word for K was and I had more important things on my mind.

"Kilo is for K," Dante informed me.

"Are we ready?" I asked. Though, under the circumstances, I was not too interested in the military language lesson; although, it was educational.

"Let's get to it!" Rocco replied, as he closed the door of the Suburban and we continued toward the destination.

"Soldiers! We will succeed; failure is not an option," Dante added.

"Grab the women and wipe out the rest," Rocco said.

"Yeah, it is go time!" Mason replied.

"Alright boys, let's cowboy up, and take care of business. Dante, you're point on this one; you're calling all the shots. Where do you want us?" I said.

"Mason and Rocco will press forward on the west sidewalk arriving in the front, while Kastle and I will be on the east sidewalk and then around to the back. We'll proceed in alert mode observing everything from the ground, up. If anything is out of the ordinary, speak up. We already know the layout inside of the warehouse; so, there is nothing but open space. When the door opens, be prepared for gunfire upon entry. We'll wait and assess the situation upon arrival and orders will be given. Okay; let's hit it," Dante said.

"Copy!" Mason, Rocco, and I replied, as we followed Dante and advanced in two by two formations in complete stealth mode. Rocco was with me, while Dante and Mason were together, in compliance with Dante's orders. Once we made it to the warehouse, we evaluated the situation. Dante and Mason went in the front, while Rocco and I went in the back.

"The front is all clear," Mason said in a soft whisper; as did everyone during the evolution.

"Copy!" Dante replied.

"The back is all clear," I said, after Dante and I surveyed the perimeter and found nothing unusual.

"Copy!" Mason replied.

"Check for explosives and confirm that doors are unlocked," Dante said, as he began checking the door.

"All clear for entry in the front," Mason replied.

"All clear for entry in the back," Dante responded.

"Mason and I will take the outer walls; Kastle and Rocco will take the middle. We go on a count of five; on my mark. Is that clear?" Dante said, and then we all responded with an appropriate answer for all of us to hear.

"Back is ready!"

"Front is ready!"

"Alright we go in five..." Dante and I crept closer and closer to the door continuing the countdown, now only seconds away. While waiting I began to pray. I lost my heart once and I did not want that to happen again. With each second, my heart beat rapidly increased. With the adrenaline intensely flowing, I felt like a timed bomb ready to explode. Once the countdown reached one, our M4's was raised prepared to fire; we were ready for whatever that was waiting for us on the other side of that door.

"...Go!" Dante said, when simultaneously the doors opened, and we cautiously enter the building. Dante went in first and I followed directly behind him, I checked behind the door and the area to the right while Dante went to the left and continued staying inches away from the wall. While Dante and Mason were advancing beside each of the walls, I joined Rocco in the middle. The entire evolution was over in a matter of seconds. The warehouse was almost empty, so there was no hiding spaces; it was a big empty space easy to see everyone in there. We found Adam in the middle of the room with his hands up in the air screaming rather loudly; while Bianca and Isabella was standing beside Isabella's car about 20 feet from Adam.

"I am unarmed and there is no one here! My gun is on the table. Don't shoot! I am unarmed; don't shoot!" As Adam was yelling, I scanned the room to find his gun and to make sure there was not anyone else inside. I noticed the warehouse had changed from the last time I had been there. The place was actually clean; the walls were painted and there were a few tables and chairs.

"It's true! He is unarmed!" Isabella immediately confirmed that he was telling the truth. Rocco and I rushed to our beautiful wives, while Mason and Dante advanced five feet from Adam where they held him at gunpoint.

"Hey baby! Are you okay?" I asked Bianca, as we embraced in a hug; as did Rocco and Isabella.

"We're fine. It's so good to see you," Bianca responded.

"Did he point a gun at either of you or even touch you?" Rocco inquired.

"No! He was hiding in the back seat and never pointed a gun at us. He explained why he had to hide in the car. He informed us that we all are in danger and this was the safest way to protect us all." Isabella replied.

"She's telling the truth! Now, will you lower your weapons; we may not have much time!" Adam yelled out. We all joined Mason and Dante while they were confronting Adam.

"I like the Dragon Skin Vests. I thought that they weren't available until next year," Adam said, as he stood there admiring the bulletproof vests that Mason had acquired for us.

"I know people. Maybe if you hadn't been a ghost for the last month, you would have one too," Mason replied, as Rocco and I stood beside them facing Adam; while the girls were behind us.

"Pat him down and then lower the weapons." I said to Dante. Once Dante got us inside, I promptly took back over the leadership role.

"That's better!" Adam replied, as he noticeably exhaled.

"Don't get too relaxed. They lowered their weapons; they didn't drop them. There are some questions that we need answers for," I quickly responded.

"Look, I know where the people who are responsible for all this are hiding; but, we need to go now. I have a boat out back that we can use. I have it all planned out," Adam stated.

"I bet you do! Where have you been for the last three weeks?" Mason asked.

"I've been running for my life!" Adam replied.

"It's awfully funny that you disappear and then Banks is blown out of the sky," Dante said with a stern voice.

"That's a real good alibi you have there. This is bullshit!" Mason added.

"Guys, hold up for a second. Rocco will you put the ladies in the car so we can talk in private. Sweetheart, I'm sorry. It will only be for a few minutes; we just have to clear up a few things," I said to Bianca. Rocco escorted our wives to the car that was inside the warehouse. He made sure they knew that it was best that they didn't hear too much and he got them to turn up the radio so we could have some privacy. Rocco returned to his previous spot beside me and we proceeded with the interrogation.

"I know where the Cottos are. We need to get them tonight; before they kill one of us," Adam said.

"I'm with Mason; he is full of shit as usual," Rocco replied.

"Of course, you don't know what the hell is going on; for our sakes I'm glad the clever gentlemen you have beside you do have a clue," Adam replied.

"Why tonight?" Dante asked.

"I got word that they were coming for me and Banks. I warned Banks and we went our separate ways. I was out of the state when the explosion happened. Instead of running for the rest of my life and reading about the deaths of all of you, I thought of a plan. I found them before they could find me and I cut a deal. I gave up my accomplices in exchange for my services in the future," Adam replied.

"You gave up your accomplices!" Dante shouted.

"Seconds ago, I was the dumb ass. You have some balls to look us in the eye and tell us that you have ratted us out," Rocco responded.

"You rat fuck!" Mason said, as he raised his gun and edged a little closer toward Adam.

"If I wouldn't have done it, you all would be dead already. Tomorrow, they plan to put someone in the hospital. While all of you are there, they will blow it up. If one of you survives or isn't there, they will keep trying until they succeed. They are thorough and ruthless. Our only shot is to go get them tonight," Adam explained.

"Where is their exact location and how many are there?" I asked Adam, attempting to get all of the information I could. This way, we could decide whether to believe him or not.

"About three miles south of here, there is a house on 137 East Jackson Street; that is where the two of them are at," Adam answered.

"I thought there are three Cotto brothers?" I said to Adam.

"The oldest is Zane Cotto; he runs everything from somewhere near South America and as far as I know, he has never been inside the United States. He sent Jose and Felipe to blow up the hospital. There is someone paying ten million dollars for every requested target that is taken out on American soil," Adam responded.

"Who told you about the ten million?" Mason asked.

"Jose and Felipe told me! This is all true; you have to believe me," Adam answered, while sounding very desperate.

"What do you know about Zane Cotto?" Dante asked.

"Not too much. I heard he is scared of flying," Adam replied.

"Rocco come with me, you guys watch him; we'll be right back," I said to the boys, as Rocco and I went outside through the back door. I called Gus to see if he could give us any information about the house on Jackson Street, the identity of the Cotto brothers, and if he could confirm any of Adam's stories to be true.

"The house is owned by a Larry Tucker, a 48 year old Jacksonville native. In the last year he had flown to St. Thomas and stayed for a week on four separate occasions. He arrived the first weekend of every third month on his previous trips. Two days ago, he flew back to St. Thomas on a one way ticket; however his other tickets were one way also."

"If Adam is telling the truth, this Larry Tucker left one day after the Cottos arrived. That's just enough time to get them set up and letting the neighbors know that they shouldn't be suspicious. What can you tell me about the location of the house and the surroundings?" I said to Gus.

"The house is located fifty yards from the water and there are surrounding houses a hundred yards north and south from the Tucker house. I know it's not much to go on, but I'll keep at it. So what are you going to do?" Gus asked.

"I don't know. I have to talk it over with the guys. What do you think?"

"Work out an escape plan before hand and go check out the situation then decide after the evaluation."

"We'll discuss it and I'll call you back."

"I'll keep trying to find pictures of the Cottos. Let me know what you decide," Gus added.

"Okay, bye." I hung up with Gus and began talking to Rocco.

"What are you thinking?" I asked Rocco.

"I'm thinking setup; but, if I'm wrong, there are still a lot of unknowns. Half of South America could be there waiting for us; we will be ducks on a pond," Rocco said, as he threw his hands up, touching on legitimate points.

"Like he said, they won't stop until we all are dead. We almost don't have a choice," I responded.

"I know you want these guys and I want them too. Adam knows what buttons to push; we can't let him force us into anything. We don't know whose side he's really on," Rocco said.

"We can go now or we can wait a day or so and devise a plan to take them out. So what do you say?" I replied.

"I'm with you; I completely support your decision," Rocco said.

"Let's go see what Dante and Mason have to say," I said, as we walked back inside the warehouse. We were immediately met with Adam yelling at the top of his lungs.

"We are running out of time!" Adam yelled. "Banks is gone. I am next in line; I should have the title now. Rocco, isn't that how the la cosa nostra works?" Adam said.

"The family decides and in our case it will never be you. In fact, without Banks, you go to the bottom of the food chain," Rocco happily responded.

"Well, we are not in Italy, New York, or New Jersey. For this group, I'm the best leader you have. If I would have been in charge, Banks' killers would already be dead and your hot wife wouldn't be in danger," Adam said, while starring at Rocco.

"That's big talk coming from someone fifty feet from their gun. Go ahead and keep talking your shit; I won't wait on an order to clip your sorry ass," Rocco replied.

"Hold on, Rocco. We have something to talk about," I said.

"No Kastle, we all gave him a pass for years because of Banks and now this piece of shit is not needed anymore. The dumb fuck has given us all of the information we need; he is now useless," Rocco replied.

"I'm sure we have your attention now," I said to Adam.

"I took it too far. I'm sorry. Now can we get to the part where we go get these guys? For the last time, I am telling the truth; I bet my life on it. I will walk up there first with no gun, no vest, and my hands tied behind my back. That is how much I trust you guys; even though you don't trust me," Adam said.

"Enough! Alright guys, what do you say? Are we going tonight or are we waiting?" I asked the boys.

"I say we go check it out tonight," Dante answered.

"Let's go get these bitches!" Mason added, as he walked up to me and gently tapped the side of my shoulder.

"I'm in; but, if you're lying, you will be 'on the lam' again, from me," Rocco said, as he glared at Adam.

"Okay, we're going. Dante get the truck. Mason, watch him; while we take care of the girls," I said, as Rocco and I walked to the car to talk to our wives. I walk to the passenger side as Rocco went to the driver's side.

"Hey baby, we have to go. We're getting Adam out of town; we will meet you two back at Banks' house." We sent the ladies off to Banks' house where they would be safe. Gus was there along with other bodyguards from RB Security to protect them if anything happened. We opened the sliding doors to the warehouse to let the girls out and let Dante in.

"I'm going to call Gus. Go ahead and get all of the gear we need and find plasticuffs for him," I said, as I started to walk outside.

"Are you seriously going to put those on me? I'm about to save the day," Adam replied, as he chuckled at what I said.

"You have to earn trust. If what you have said is true, you can gradually gain ours throughout the night. Until then, the plasticuffs stay on," I answered.

"Whatever it takes for us to get on that boat; I'll do it," Adam responded, as I walked outside and called Gus.

"It's a go! We're going to check it out and if we need back up we'll call; I'll let you know when it's over. We sent Bianca and Isabella back to you, so they will be protected. Do you have any pictures of the Cottos yet?" I said to Gus.

"Yes. I was just about to send them," Gus replied.

"Send them to all of us. Except, send me pictures of the two of them and three different guys. I want to see if Adam can pick them out of a lineup," I said.

"Consider it done. Kastle?" Gus responded.

"Yeah!"

"Good luck to you guys and take care of yourselves," Gus said.

"I'll call when it's done; take care of my wife." I hung up with Gus and joined the others at the boat.

Chapter 14
Hello Cotto

We all boarded the boat with our gear and made preparations to cast off. We all received the pictures from Gus and I instantly went up to Adam. I wanted him to be able to show me which two of the five pictures, on my phone, were of Jose and Felipe Cotto. The two that Adam picked were the same pictures that were on Rocco's phone. It was now confirmed; we were, now, in business. After that was determined, Dante started the boat and had us on our way.

"Alright, Adam, where exactly are we going?" I asked Adam.

"Take this off my wrists and I'll tell you," Adam answered.

"What are you reneging, already?" I responded.

"Tell us, before we deep-six your ass," Mason said.

"Okay, three miles south of here, there is a fishing pier where we can dock the boat. The house can be seen from there," Adam replied. Mason revealed a black bag and began to hand out silencers to everyone.

"We could have used these earlier," I said to Mason.

"I didn't think we needed this in the warehouse," Mason responded.

"Well, maybe not," I replied, even though I felt we did.

We arrived at the dock a few minutes later. We, immediately, began to observe the house thru binoculars. I looked at the house and there were no lights on. I then began to scan the entire property area. There was a shed about twenty yards from the house; and houses on both sides, fifty to seventy-five yards from the house.

"Are you sure this is the right house?' I asked Adam.

"This is it! I told you that we had to hurry; but no, you guys had to screw around. You should have listened and all of this would be done with." Adam responded.

"What do you say, let's at least go check it out?" I said into the microphone to all of the guys.

"Yeah, let's do it," somebody replied. We were talking softly, so I couldn't recognize who it was.

"Mason and Dante go ahead; Rocco and I will cover you. When you get there, we'll join you with cover."

"Can I be unrestrained now?" Adam pleaded, as he was becoming more agitated by the second.

"There is no proof that they are here; this could still be a setup," I replied, as Dante and Mason take off to the storage shed.

"You'll see. I hope we're not too late," Adam said.

"Yeah, me too; now, come with us," I said. The three of us made our way down the pier and then to the shed behind the house. There was a white van parked beside the storage shed.

"There is a van missing; there was two here earlier. They must be gone," Adam said, giving us information to support his so called truth.

"Let's see if we can find any explosives while we are here. Dante, you and Mason check the van and we'll look in the shed. Be careful," I said, as we quickly began our tasks. From what I have gathered, Mason and Dante were the most experienced dealing with explosives; and, definitely, the most qualified should be the first ones in. Banks gave me a crash course with explosives during my training period; but, at that point, the more experienced operatives should be dealing with a live bomb. While they were inspecting the van, we did the same in the shed. The three of us walked around the shed to the front door. As Rocco opened the door, Dante confirmed that there was a bomb in the van.

"We have a bomb, there's over a hundred pounds of C4 in here," Dante said.

"Did you say a hundred pounds?" Rocco asked in astonishment.

"At least!" Dante replied.

"It looks like we found our guys," Rocco replied.

"These cuffs are pretty tight! Can you take them off and let me lend a hand," Adam said.

"We haven't seen anyone yet; the cuffs are staying on," I replied, even though his story was becoming more believable.

"You'll see. Everything I have said is true," Adam said.

"Check the house. We'll be right behind you, when we're done in here," I said, as I walked through the door of the shed.

"Copy that," Mason replied. Once inside of the shed, we broke out our pocket flash lights and began to explore the area; and it didn't take long for us to find what we were looking for.

"I have a trunk full of detonators over here," I said.

"I've got plastic explosives in crates over here. There's got to be over two hundred pounds of C4 in there," Rocco responded.

"I told you! Now do you trust me?" Adam said.

"Fuck no! We don't trust you. Now shut the fuck up!" Rocco replied, as he covered his microphone.

"Dante and Mason did you catch that?" I asked.

"C4 and detonators; we copy," one of them answered. They were talking softly again, while they were in the house.

"I'm going to the van to be on look out for the guys," Rocco said.

"Alright, I'll be out in a second. Take him with you," I replied, as Rocco began to escort Adam outside.

"Will you stop treating me like a prisoner and admit that I've been right?" Adam said, as he reached the door.

"Not yet!" Rocco replied, as he walked behind him. I continued look around while everyone else had everything under control. I investigated every inch of the space for any useful evidence. I did not find anything appealing; only the C4 and the detonators. I found a plastic bag that I used to put a small block of C4 and a detonator in. I was thinking that maybe Gus could trace where it all came from. I knew it was a long shot, but it didn't hurt to try; even though he would probably laugh in my face. I took the evidence and headed to the door.

"We're all clear in here," Dante said, after I exited the shed.

"Let's wait for them; it will be best to get them in the house. How many more bodies do you need?" I said.

"Dunn, are you up for this?" Dante asked Mason.

"Yeah, let's do it Jacks. We got this in here," Mason replied.

"We've got our infrared goggles. They won't know what hit `em," Dante responded.

"Okay, it is all yours. In the mean time, just hang tight fellas and we'll give you the heads up when they arrive. Meanwhile, I'll call Gus to let him know to keep everyone over there on lockdown, until we give the okay," I said. I immediately dialed Gus and I informed him of the situation, as well as, our plan. He agreed with our decision and assured me no one would leave until we give the word. I got off the phone and joined Rocco and Adam behind the shed. When I arrived, I found the two of them sitting down leaning against the wall of the shed and surprisingly there wasn't any bickering going on.

"It's good to see you two getting along," I said.

"Yeah, we are best pals," Adam replied. I couldn't see, but I knew that they were rolling there eyes.

"Okay, let's take our positions at our lookout points and get ready to end this; so, we can get this one out of his plasticuffs," Rocco said.

"That's the smartest and the nicest thing I've ever heard you say," Adam replied.

"Don't get used to me being nice; I am just tired of being this close to you," Rocco responded. He and Adam rose up from their sitting position and went off to man there post, together. Rocco and I found good locations, about twenty yards from the house, to set up; which put us in an excellent position to attack, if necessary.

"How are you two doing in the house?" I asked.

"We're good; just waiting on the action," Mason replied. We continued to, patiently, wait. About the thirty minute mark, we finally saw some activity. There was a white cargo van that was braking and finally turned in the driveway. The van eased up the driveway and came to a complete stop around ten feet from the house.

"We have confirmation. The subjects are in the van," I said over the radio, after I was able to get a good look at them.

"Copy. The targets have been confirmed," Mason responded.

"Shooters have a green light," Rocco replied.

"Affirmative!" Dante responded.

"Targets are exiting the vehicle, ten feet from the door." Rocco said, as he gave the guys the standard protocol; a play by play.

"Infrared goggles are on; awaiting targets." Dante whispered as the Cotto brothers walked closer to the door. They were talking loudly and stumbling a little; you could tell that they had been drinking. I could not make out what they were saying; I only caught a few words that lead me to believe they just came from a strip club. I heard one of them say, "dance" and "tits," from which I drew my conclusion.

"Targets at the door; prepare to engage." Rocco continued his commentating for the guys on the inside. The two entered the house. I could not see anything, but I heard the Cotto brothers say something about the lights, that were previously cut by Dante and Mason. As the door shut, we advanced toward the house. A couple of seconds later, there was activity over the radio.

"All clear; it's done!" Mason announced. Afterwards, we entered the house and joined the guys.

"Let's get these bodies to the boat," I said. I went up to Adam and cut his plasticuffs. "Now you're free!"

"Finally!" Adam said.

"Great, no more babysitting!" Rocco replied.

"Finally, I can say I told you so. Are you guys ever going to give me any credit?" Adam responded.

"When we're home free, you'll get a pat on the back," Dante said to Adam, as we began to carry the bodies out of the house and to the boat. It was the first time I had ever touched a dead body; I was really freaked out. It was truly creepy to have a dead human being in my hands that was alive a few seconds before. It was a first time experience that took a little time to deal with; I realized quickly that I did not have the stomach to work at a mortuary. I blocked out my thoughts concerning the corpse and continued on with the task at hand. We reached the boat with the Cottos and prepared to cast off.

I called Gus to give him the good news and to let him know about the explosives. I told him to give us at least an hour before he called in an anonymous tip to the authorities. He informed me that they would get a tip sometime in the following morning. We departed from the pier and began to contemplate where to dispose of the bodies. We all surprisingly agreed with Adam's suggestion and headed to Suge Island. On the way, we put the bodies in body bags.

Upon arriving there, it seemed different than from what I had remembered. Adam provided an explanation of the change.

"Do you like what I've done to the place? I have been hiding out here for some of the time I was gone. I have something we can use for weights inside, follow me." We broke out our flashlights and followed Adam into the shack.

"With all the money you have, you stayed here?" Mason said, as Adam picked up cement blocks and started handing them out.

"Fuck this, we don't need weights; the sharks will probably eat their asses anyway," Rocco said.

"You have been awfully quiet. I am still waiting for a thank you or something," Adam said to Rocco.

"I'm stunned that you came through, for once; now, pass me the fucking blocks so we can get out of here," Rocco responded.

"Come on let's get this over with," I replied, as we all carried blocks back to the boat and put a chain through the blocks that wrapped around the bag. We left the island and after about ten miles out; Dante stopped the boat and we jettisoned the bodies. What a relief that was to get rid of that extra weight; it was an out of sight, out of mind type of thing. We arrived back at the warehouse, where Dante was going to drop us off while he stashed the boat somewhere. I was the last one to get off before Dante took off.

"Kastle, here's my keys; I'll call you to pick me up when I find a good spot to dump this," Dante said, as he threw me his keys.

"Come inside for a second, there's something important we all need to discuss." I replied.

"Alright, I'm right behind you," Dante responded, as he stepped off the boat. We all went into the warehouse and began to put our gear into Dante's suburban.

"So, what's next?" Adam asked, as he was inspecting Mason's Dragon Skin by rubbing his hand over the outer portion of the very intriguing vest.

"We go after everyone who was involved with all of this: the school bombing and Banks' death. We end it!" I replied.

"Do you think you will be able to handle, not being in charge?" Mason asked Adam.

"Can you be a team player?" Dante said, as he turned and looked at Adam.

"Will you take orders and not be such a pain in my ass?" Rocco added, as he closed the back of the suburban.

"The answer is, yes, to all of that. I thought, after tonight, you guys could see what a stand up guy I am," Adam responded, mainly looking at Rocco while he was speaking.

"I'll admit that you have taken positive steps in being considered as a family guy," Rocco said, mildly giving Adam a little credit.

"Okay, that is good enough for me. The five of us are a team. In our circle there's nothing we won't accomplish; taking care of business, by any means necessary. Now, we are all regular civilians that will stand up for what we believe in. We will find everyone responsible for the bombings and stop anyone by lethal force who tries to harm us or anyone in our great country. You guys have saluted the flag vowing to defend this country, and now I ask to let me stand beside you and take an oath; with hand over heart, terrorism will cease when we are done." I emphatically said, getting everyone's full attention.

"We should help out while our boys are at war. I'm with you," Dante responded.

"That was pretty good; sounds like you are running for president," Adam replied.

"No, that was damn good. I'm ready for combat," Dante responded.

"I can tell, without a doubt, that your blood is indeed red, white, and blue." Mason added.

"The head of the family has spoken. We're behind you Kastle," Rocco acknowledged.

"I guess, now, I have to change my tattoo from a B to a K," Adam said.

"There you go with the tattoo again," Rocco replied, as I handed him two plasticuffs.

"We're a team and we are all equal. Each of us will be doing this for a cause that we believe in. If anyone wants no part of this, now is the time to go our separate ways?" I replied.

"We are all in," Mason said, as everyone else agreed with him.

"Adam, do you agree?" I asked just to make sure that I heard his answer clearly.

"Yes, I am. There will be no stopping this team," Adam replied.

"Adam, come sit down in this chair; there's a small initiation we do before you are officially apart of the team. Rocco, a little help," I said, as Rocco put the restraints around the arm rest of the chair and around Adam's wrists.

"What initiation?" Mason asked, while I could tell that the other guys had the same question on their minds.

"Kastle, what's going on?" Dante asked, as we all walked up to Adam and joined Rocco standing in front of him.

"I just want answers; if you give them to us, it will be the last time we will ever tie you up," I said.

"What is this about?" Adam surprisingly asked.

"Oh you know! So go ahead and talk; before we have to get into it," I replied.

"Get into what? I have told you all everything," Adam said in a pleading voice; while I noticed that he was missing something.

"Where is your yoyo?" I asked, as I noticed a piece of a string tied around his middle finger on his right hand.

"I don't need it anymore. All I need for stress management is this string around my finger," Adam answered, as everyone looked at his finger.

"Rocco you have always wanted to get your hands on him; now, here's your chance," I said, while looking at Rocco.

"Are you serious?" Rocco asked, in total disbelief.

"Go ahead and hit him; and, if he won't talk, pound on him until he does," I replied.

"Whoa! This is like Christmas," Rocco responded with a huge smile on his face.

"I have no idea what you are talking about," Adam said.

"Wait! Kastle, what's up? Why are we going to watch Rocco beat on our friend? He is one of us!" Dante said.

"Our friend here had better start talking. Just trust me," I said to Dante.

"I have told you all everything. I believe after tonight I have shown that I can be trusted, but can you? You said that we are a team and that we are equal," Adam replied.

"I know for a fact that there is something that you are not telling us. If you really want to be a part of this team, you will speak now and come clean about everything," I said, starring down at Adam.

"Rocco at least smack him in the mouth one good time," Mason replied.

"Rock his ass!" I added, moments before Rocco stuck him in the mouth. Afterwards, you could see a look of satisfaction on Rocco's face; I was happy for him. I knew he had been waiting to do that for so long.

"Oh, that felt good!" Rocco replied, even though he had no idea what my reasons were. He could not resist doing something that he had wanted to do for years.

"Nice shot! Now, do you have anything that you what like to tell us?" I said to Adam.

"I hope not; I would love to do it again," Rocco replied.

"You are going to have to pound on me; because I don't know anything," Adam replied, after he took a pretty good lick from Rocco.

"Do remember me telling you guys that I saw him and Ponce in Miami. They looked real cozy together; like they would do anything for each other," I said.

"Hey, fuck you! I never liked him! I was only around him for business," Adam furiously replied.

"Wrong answer! Who has a knife? I think his hand should match his good buddy Ponce. Rocco; the left pinky," I said, as Rocco walked up to Adam with his knife in his hand.

"Smacking him around is one thing, but hacking off a finger is something different. Are you sure you're right?" Rocco said.

"Banks left folders to all of us in a safe; just in case anything ever happened to him. In my folder, there were credit card statements with your name on it. On the day before the shipment was hijacked, you bought the same boat radio that you had to throw in the water," I said.

"You dumb fuck! You used your own credit card," Rocco replied.

"I bought a hand radio and the store clerk must have rung up the wrong radio. I know we all haven't seen eye to eye on everything, but I am telling the truth. I had nothing to do with that. You have to believe me. I have proof back at my house," Adam said.

"You are off your rocker if you think I'm going to allow you to slither out of this," Rocco replied.

"You know, I thought it was weird that you wanted to unload the shipment by yourself and give up millions so easily, for your so called fuck up," Dante replied.

"What did you get out of the shipment? How much did you get for fucking us over?" Mason asked.

"You should really say something. I'm now looking forward to chopping off your digits," Rocco said.

"Now is the time to start talking; you are in quite a predicament," Mason replied, as I walked over to Dante's Suburban and got the bag with the C4 and the detonators out of it. I then go over to Dante and give him the C4. I hand the detonator to Mason and gave the plastic bag to Rocco.

"Do you guys see anything that can be linked to that particular shipment?" I asked the guys, as I saw Rocco put his hand in the bag and pulled it out, then brought his up to his face. He saw a substance on his finger, which he then licked.

"This is coke!" Rocco said, as the others did the same.

"The bags could have come from anywhere, that doesn't mean that all of that is from that shipment. As far as I knew, there was only coke in the shipment that was jacked. I know nothing about all of this," Adam responded.

"Fuck the fingers! I'm going to hack off your nuts. Consider everything down there permanently fucked," Rocco replied.

"You are so full of shit! Come clean or I will take your whole fucking hand off," Dante said, as he got closer to Adam.

"Fuck this!" Mason said, as he punches Adam in the face three times.

"Wait! I have something I want to say to him." Dante said, as he moves Mason out of the way and then he too punches Adam.

"You know, there is something I have been curious about," I said. I started to take off the Dragon Skin Body Armor that I was wearing. "I want to know if a person wearing this can really lay on a grenade and walk away unharmed," I said, as I threw my vest to Mason.

"That's a great idea," Mason quickly responded.

"I want to see that myself," Rocco said, with a huge smile on his face, while Mason was putting the body armor on Adam.

"I do to. It will be a test we can use for future reference," Dante replied. Although, he made it sound like he didn't really believe, that we would go threw with it.

"You dumb asses don't think that I am going to just lay on top of a grenade, do you?" Adam responded.

"We can rig up something to keep you on it; or we can put the grenade down your shirt and see if the Dragon Skin will keep the blast contained," Mason said, as he returned to his previous position in front of Adam and beside us.

"Okay! Yes, I gave the shipment to Ponce, but I didn't know there was C4 stashed in the coke. He threatened me; if I didn't do it I would be dead and so would all of you. I did what I thought was best. I had to stay alive to warn everyone what was going on. I'm so sorry for this; that is why I gave you guys your cut from the shipment," Adam said, giving us an explanation for his actions.

"A couple of 'I'm sorry's' is not enough. You are not going to skate on this. So how much did you get?" I asked Adam.

"Nothing, you can ask Gus to check my account."

"He's lying!" Rocco replied.

"Fuck you, Rocco. Like you guys are so innocent in all this. We were putting cocaine on the streets." Adam said, as I noticed him moving his restrained right hand like he was playing with an invisible yoyo.

"You stabbed us in the back. You fuck!" Rocco replied.

"...And you put C4 in a school," I responded, as I had goose bumps; which usually occurred every time I thought about the unthinkable events of that tragic day.

"...And Banks' plane," Dante added. By this time I had enough. I walked over to Adam and shot him in his hand with my 9mm. Adam immediately cries out in pain.

"Tell us everything!" I screamed, as I took a step back from the chair.

"We have a lot more body parts to put a bullet in," Dante added.

"Okay! I was in deep with Ponce. He told me to bring the shipment to a location and I would get a cut for it. I thought I could make us more money; but, for the time being, I didn't want to get you involved. So, I told you all that it was jacked and I gave everyone their original cut. Plus, Banks would have killed me if he knew that I was doing a deal with Ponce. I never saw a dime from Ponce. He told me he had another job he had to finish; then, I would get paid."

"How much?" Rocco asked.

"Twenty million! I didn't know anything about the shipment or the job he had to do," Adam answered.

"You fucking cocksucker. You knew about the school bombing," Rocco replied.

"You bed down with the enemy," Dante added.

"It is more like he was taking it in the ass," Mason said, as he glared at Adam's conniving mug.

"I didn't find out until the morning of. I didn't know what to do," Adam said, as he started to get emotional; his eyes began to tear up.

"You could have called Sarah! You could have called in a fucking bomb threat!" I said in an outrage.

"I tried to call her, but I couldn't get an answer; it went straight to voice mail. I called Banks to tell him that Ponce wanted me to find a plane to fly him to South America. I didn't know when the bomb was set to go off, so I headed to the school. A couple of minutes after I hung up with Banks the explosion happened. I was over ten miles away. There was nothing I could do, but try to find Ponce and give the location to you guys." Adam responded, as he was continuously sobbing at this point.

"Well, Ponce is not around to corroborate your story, is he?" Mason said.

"You little bitch, and you popped him before he could rat you out!" I responded.

"I have been saying for years that you are a rat fuck and I never trusted your pathetic ass," Rocco said, as he drew closer to Adam.

"We just stood here and said we will get everyone responsible, and all of this is because of you. You brought Ponce and his brothers to us and because you were in bed with them; Banks and Sarah are gone. All of those kids are gone because of you," I said, as I took one step closer towards Adam.

"There is more to it! There is something big planned, that I couldn't find out about. Ponce would always say, that in the future I would want to be on their side," Adam said, in somewhat of desperation with a tear falling occasionally.

"And you chose their side!" Dante replied, as he drew closer to Adam.

"No, I didn't!" Adam responded.

"You chose when you put a bullet in Ponce, before he could tell us about the big thing he was talking about. You chose to cover your own ass and, consequently, choosing the same fate, you motherfucker. I don't know how close you all are; so I will understand if anyone wants to sit this one out," I said, looking at Mason and especially Dante. I already knew where Rocco stood.

"He deserves what's coming and then some," Dante said, as we all raised our guns.

"Wait! I really want to do the grenade test." I said.

"I'm curious too; but, it has been a long day," Rocco replied.

"I'm all for it; I'll even take care of the body myself afterwards," Mason said.

"Adam was one of us at one time; he wasn't always like this. He deserves a bullet in the head; but no grenade," Dante said.

"I agree, Mason. We'll do the test when we come across the last Cotto brother," I said, as I began to take my vest off of Adam.

"No, don't do this. I can find Zane Cotto; face it, you guys need me." Adam said pleading with us, as I now stood beside Mason and the rest of the guys with my vest in my left hand.

"What we need is this!" I said, as we each put a couple of rounds in Adam's chest.

"We're going to find out this big plan for the future and we're going to stop it. We may not get to every terrorist; but, we will do our part," I said, a few seconds after the last shot was fired.

"Yes we are!" Without question, Rocco and the guys completely agreed with me.

Chapter 15
It Rains in New York

A couple of weeks later, I accompanied Bianca to New York. Gus and the guys were trying to get information from their contacts and other sources. However, they produced nothing, up to that point. After considering that, I figured it would not hurt to get out of town for a few days. So, I took a little time to spend with my wife and accompanied her to New York on a business trip.

Once we arrived at our hotel on the first day in New York, I finally got around to having the talk about Adam and that entire situation. I was hesitant on having that discussion. If she knew that our lives were in danger, I was almost certain, I would lose her; but, I had to warn her, regardless of what it cost me.

"We need to sit down. There is something we need to discuss," I said, as I put our luggage down and I went to sit down on the bed. I figured it was better to go ahead and get it over with, before I unpacked my bag.

"Wait; let me go to the bathroom first. I'll be right out," Bianca said, as she walked in the bathroom and closed the door.

"Okay!" I replied, as I turned on the TV and began to watch Sports Center. When she came out of the bathroom she walked to me and sat beside me on the bed.

"Okay, what would you like to talk about?" Bianca asked me. I, then, turned off the TV.

"Well, we haven't really talked about Adam and that whole situation," I said.

"I have been curious, but I wanted you to come to me. I received an orientation speech from Isabella and the runaround on every question that I asked," she said.

"Adam got involved with some dangerous people and they were looking for him; he needed our help to disappear. I'm sorry he involved you. He is now out of the country and he's never coming back."

"I was scared when he first popped his head up in the backseat; but, I quickly discovered that I wasn't in danger," she replied.

"I love you and I want to protect you from any danger," I said.

"I believe you can do that. I've seen you do that," Bianca replied.

"My boss and his daughter died, and they didn't know that they were in danger. I want to spend the rest of my life with you, but I have to give you that option."

"Isabella told me about Sarah and how hurt you were; how hurt you all were. I want us to be together forever. Are we in any danger?" There was a few seconds of silence when I didn't answer her. "Isabella also told me that her husband and the other guys that were with you in the warehouse were all in the military together. She said that when he would go on top secret, Special Forces missions and come home, he would act a certain way. She would never ask what he did or where he went; she just wanted him to come home alive. In the four years that her husband has been out of the military; she had not seen that look from him until you came along. So, let me rephrase my previous question. Am I in any danger?"

"No, you are not," I replied. Well, at that point in time, in Manhattan, I did not believe that she was in any danger.

"I love you! Will you keep us safe and make us a living, along with my contribution of course, with a legitimate business?"

"Yes, I will," I said, as I leaned over and kissed her.

"Okay. That is all I needed to know," Bianca replied.

"Are you sure you don't want to know everything? I have been struggling with this for the past couple of weeks. That is why I haven't talked to you about the Adam before now," I said, as I put my arm around her.

"No. That is about all we can handle for the moment," Bianca replied.

"Well, I am going to write everything down on paper and put it in the safe; and if you ever want to know, you can read it. I don't want to hide anything from you. I care about you too much. So we are all good?" I asked.

"Yes, of course," Bianca said, as she leaned over and kissed me.

"Good, because I have something planned for you on our way back home."

"You can go ahead and tell me; I don't want anymore surprises," she replied.

"Okay, if that is what you want. Since we're not too far away; I'm taking you to Pittsburg to visit the dance studio in *Flashdance*," which is Bianca's all time favorite movie; she absolutely loves it. The first time I rode in her car, she was listening to the soundtrack, where she occasionally sang along word for word.

"That is so sweet, but you are too late; Tristan took me and Sophie there last year," she responded.

"Great minds think alike! Well, that's disappointing. I was going to have a half dozen roses and a stuffed dog waiting for you when you came outside," I replied. It shocked me to find out that she had already been there; as much as she talked about it, she had never mentioned it before. I was crushed. I really thought that I was going to score some major points with that one.

"It's okay to be late sometimes; I'm late too," Bianca said, as she began to tear up, while she cracked a huge smile.

Wait! What did you mean by late?" I asked Bianca, as she continued to smile.

"So do you remember all the times I had to pee in the airport, on the plane, and just a few minutes ago? Well, I wasn't peeing. I took a pregnancy test as soon as we got in here, and it said that I am pregnant."

"Really?" I replied as we hugged and I kissed her. If it was true, that was definitely one of the greatest moments of my life.

"Yes! It is not definite though; I still have to see a doctor," she responded, as she began to cry.

"Oh, baby, I am so happy! I love you so much!" I said to her, as I kissed her again and again. There was a lot of kissing going on for the rest of the night and for the next couple of days.

"I am happy too!" Bianca replied. The next day she saw a doctor in New York and he confirmed that we were going to have a baby.

Two days later, she had a meeting over lunch in Manhattan, not too far from "Ground Zero." While she was at lunch, I was going to walk around and she was going to call me when she was done. It was raining that day, so I had to buy an umbrella. I made it to the construction site at "Ground Zero," I wanted to see how much progress had been made since I was last there. I, then, began to think of what all had happened in the last couple of months and even the last year or so. As I stood there deep in thought, I saw someone out of the corner of my eye not too far away from me. I turn to my right and all I could see was a person with a blue umbrella, with a New York Yankee logo on it; I couldn't see a face. A few seconds later the person walked closer to me as the umbrella was lifted up revealing the persons identity; it was Sarah.

"Oh my God! I have to be dreaming," I said, as she touches my hand.

"It's me! I've wanted, for so long, to see you and touch you," Sarah replied.

"How did you get out? Why are you here?" I asked in amazement.

"Everything happened so fast; there was nothing I could do. My dad called me and told me to walk outside and go to my car. I only got maybe a block away when the explosion occurred. I was crushed at that point; I feel bad every second for all of the kids that were in there that I didn't help," she replied.

"There wasn't enough time; there was nothing you could do," I replied.

"That day I lost everything; I lost my life, I lost you. I met up with my dad a couple hours later and he notified me of the situation and we decided my only option was to disappear. He set it up so no one knew about it and I would be safe. I only had one request before I agreed to take on a new life; to say goodbye to you somewhere down the line and to warn you all of the danger," Sarah said.

"So you have a new name and a new identity," I responded, still in disbelief.

"Yes, but I can't tell you what it is; and we can never see each other again. Everyone in my old life doesn't exist. I couldn't even go to my dad's funeral. He was trying to keep us all safe and he gets killed anyway. I cry at least once a day; for either him, or for you, or even for no reason. I did get to see you once, before now. I saw you on TV at the Laker game. My dad called me and told me to watch the game; it was the only time I have ever cried while watching a basketball game. I cried again when I heard you had gotten married and I will cry when I walk away from you for the last time. I am so glad that you found happiness, maybe I can find the same in my new life; but I want you to know that you will always have a piece of me," Sarah said, as a tear or two were falling down her cheeks.

"I feel the same way about you," I said, as I looked into her eyes.

"Sometimes, I regret my choice, but my dad was sure that there was danger for everyone around him then and in the future."

"What do you have to warn me about?" I asked.

"You and all the guys are in danger, my dad found out the truth about Zane Cotto. Adam is really Zane Cotto; Adam Marshall doesn't exist. He took on the identity of Adam Marshall before he started working as a bodyguard for my dad. My dad discovered this and Adam blew him out of the sky. He was on his way to tell you everything when his plane went down," Sarah responded. I couldn't believe what she had said; it totally blew my mind. I began to piece everything together to have it all make sense.

"I thought Adam was in the military with Banks."

"No, my Dad wanted him to fit in with the guys, so he just told everybody that he was in the Army. Zane Cotto had everyone fooled and when my Dad finally found out the truth about him, he was killed," Sarah replied.

"Are you sure?" I asked.

"Yes! They say Zane Cotto used a string to strangle his father; and he kept a piece of that string tied around his middle finger on his right hand as a reminder of the torture sessions he and his brothers went through," Sarah said.

"Really?" I said in complete shock.

"Yes, my Dad called me to warn me that Adam or Zane could know that I was still alive and I could still be in more danger; when all along he was the one in danger. You need to find Adam and make him tell you everything," Sarah replied, as she confirmed that everything she said was true; which was an enormous relief, but to be on the safe side I was definitely going to check into it and make sure.

"Fuck me!" I said.

"What?" Sarah replied.

"I can't ask Adam anything; he went one on one with a shark in the exact place that Banks' plane went down," I responded.

"I'm glad to hear it. He deserved that and much more for everything that he has done," Sarah said, while the pain she was feeling was easily visible; I felt for her. As for me, a life of enjoyment, normalcy, and raising a family in a safe environment could now be a welcomed reality.

"How do you know all of this?" I curiously asked. It was just hard for me to believe that Adam was Zane Cotto. I guess I had built an image of Zane in my head as a dangerous and ruthless individual; when he or any terrorist for that matter is really just an everyday, regular, weak coward once their identity is revealed.

"My dad told me all of this when he called me, just before he left to see you," she responded.

"Thank you for telling me all of this. I'm so glad you are alive; I wish this would not have happened. I..." I said, before Sarah abruptly cut me off.

"Stop! It's done, and we can't go back. I have to go or I never will. I pray that you will have a full, safe, and enjoyable life. Take care of yourself. I will always love you," Sarah said, as the tears continued to fall down her cheek.

"I love you too," I replied, as Sarah walked away. I continued to stand there shocked at what had just occurred, wrapping my head around all of the information that I had just received. Seconds later, I am startled by a grab of my arm. I turned to my right and found Bianca standing there.

"Oh, hey baby. This place gets me into another world every time," I responded.

"I thought I would find you here. Are you ready to go?" She asked.

"Yes, I am ready to go home. I love you so much," I replied, as I held Bianca's hand and we began to walk away. I held the umbrella up for the both of us.

"I love you too. Who was the Yankee fan that you were talking to when I walked up?" She asked.

"Oh, just a woman that lost someone special here," I answered. I put my arm around her as we continued to walk in the rain, getting closer, with every step, to what the future had in store for us.

Castle Doctrine-The state of Florida in the United States became the first to enact the Castle Doctrine (or Castle Law) on October 1, 2005. The Florida statute allows the use of deadly force when a person reasonably believes it necessary to prevent the commission of a "forcible felony." Under the statute, forcible felonies include "treason; murder; manslaughter; carjacking; home-invasion robbery; kidnapping; aircraft piracy; unlawful throwing, placing, or discharging of a destructive device or bomb, and other felony which involves the use or threat of physical force or violence against any individual."

CHRIS COPELAND

www.ingramcontent.com/pod-product-compliance
Lightning Source LLC
Chambersburg PA
CBHW050929120626
46552CB00001B/111